Story Of The Storey

Blindfold Arises

K B Janaki

Chennai • Bangalore

CLEVER FOX PUBLISHING
Chennai, India

Published by CLEVER FOX PUBLISHING 2025
Copyright © K B Janaki 2025

All Rights Reserved.
ISBN: 978-93-6707-679-8

This book has been published with all reasonable efforts taken to make the material error-free after the consent of the author. No part of this book shall be used, reproduced in any manner whatsoever without written permission from the author, except in the case of brief quotations embodied in critical articles and reviews.

The Author of this book is solely responsible and liable for its content including but not limited to the views, representations, descriptions, statements, information, opinions and references ["Content"]. The Content of this book shall not constitute or be construed or deemed to reflect the opinion or expression of the Publisher or Editor. Neither the Publisher nor Editor endorse or approve the Content of this book or guarantee the reliability, accuracy or completeness of the Content published herein and do not make any representations or warranties of any kind, express or implied, including but not limited to the implied warranties of merchantability, fitness for a particular purpose. The Publisher and Editor shall not be liable whatsoever for any errors, omissions, whether such errors or omissions result from negligence, accident, or any other cause or claims for loss or damages of any kind, including without limitation, indirect or consequential loss or damage arising out of use, inability to use, or about the reliability, accuracy or sufficiency of the information contained in this book.

To my husband, **Sriram**
who urged me to write
and saw the story in me before I did.

To my parents, **Dr KVB & Kamal**
who made me believe I could
with every quiet act of love and faith.

To my mentor, **Sridevi Srinivasan**,
who didn't just say, "You can,"
but stood beside me and said, "We are doing it."

May every dreamer find someone like her
a voice of courage, steady and sure.

Acknowledgement

I whisper my first thanks to my late brother, **Mr K B Bhaskaran**. He took me wandering down forgotten lanes. In their dust the seed of this story stirred.

To my parents **Dr K. V. Balasubramanian** and **Mrs V. Kamala**, I offer a gratitude wide as the sky.

They placed books in my small hands and said, *"Reading never wounds; the mind you make afterward is what matters."* Those words lit a lantern that still burns. My father's generous foreword shines beside it.

My husband, Mr Sriram Krishnamoorthy, stood at the threshold of every doubt and whispered, "Write." He breathed life into the title. It feels part of every page and names the soul of this work. His steadfast faith was a silent pillar. It gave this novel its backbone and made it rise unshakable into being.

When shadows of uncertainty fell across a chapter, he offered patient ears and gentle guidance. He turned each stumbling block into a stepping stone. To him, I offer my deepest thank, for believing, supporting, and walking beside me every step of the way.

Acknowledgement

Silence is a rare gift. My parents-in-law, **Mrs K. Vasantha** and **Mr S. Krishnamoorthy**, wrapped our home in it. So, I could hear the rhythm of my own sentences.

Laughter is rarer still. My son, **Mr S. Vidhur J. Adidev**, scattered it like sunlight on the desk where I worked. Each giggle became a line break, each smile a fresh page.

Guidance came on careful feet. My aunt, **Mrs Kamala Murali**, and my mentor, **Dr B. V. Saraswathy**, read, corrected, and polished until rough stone showed a hint of jewel.

The first path to wonder was opened by my cousin **Vishalakshi Muralidharan**. She pressed a novel into my palms long ago, and the world tilted toward possibility.

For years the plot drifted like mist scribbles nested in a digital keep, scenes half-dreamed. Then **Sridevi Srinivasan** arrived with steady faith. The mist became rain, and the rain became chapters. It was her who urged me to give voice to these pages With equal generosity, lent her own pen to write its foreword.

Acknowledgement

This book is woven from footsteps, heartbeats, and quiet breaths held tight. If you sense its rhythm, know it carries the echoes of many lives. I am grateful to every soul who journeyed with me to bring these pages to life.

Foreword

Dr. K.V. Balasubramanian,
M.Sc., M.A. (Tamil & His), M. Phil., Ph. D.
Retired Meteorologist,
No. 2, First Floor, Kannabiran koil street,
Perambur, Chennai-11
Mobile-9884715004
Email – kvbmanian@yahoo.com

Smt. Janaki Sriram, M.A., B. Ed., M. Phil., is my daughter, and it is a pleasure to write a foreword to her first book. Having known her from childhood, I must confess that I never thought that she would be writing a book. Every time a major exam approached, she would fall sick, and I would be taking her to a hospital for treatment. Once, the doctor asked what the problem was, and I said that she has exams tomorrow. Such a person has studied up to M.A., B.Ed., M. Phil. that itself is a great achievement.

When she was studying for her B.A. (English), she developed an interest in reading books. Naturally, I suggested some books to her. But she had her own preferences. She was very fond of retelling myths. Then, she wanted to do some work in "travelogues".

Foreword

Here, too, she used to discuss this with me. Her M. Phil. Dissertation was on the travel writing of Shri Biswanath Ghosh. One of the books she chose for study was "Aimless in Banaras". After submitting the dissertation, I took her to Varanasi to have a feel of the city.

She was writing a book on English Grammar, which has been completed and is with the publisher. It is getting delayed for release at the publisher's end, and in the meantime, this novel is ready for publication.

She has lived in Madhavaram, Tabalpetti; studied in Chevalier T Thomas Elizabeth College for Women. These are mentioned in the novel. Nowadays, she is associated with Little Laudable Learners, an institution that imparts knowledge to little kids through online mode. It also is mentioned in the novel.

For the past few years, I have stopped reading books. At best, I read newspapers, Kumudham, Ananda Vikatan. Most of my reading is through my laptop only. Recently, I had been to Janaki's house. While returning, I asked her to give me a book to read in the train, and she gave me one. I have not completed the book yet.

But this novel I finished reading within about three hours. The novel is nice. The language is fine and elegant. The events are well connected. I

Foreword

don't want to give a gist of the story here, because it will dampen your spirits while reading the book. The novel is a thriller a ghost story; a murder investigation; the history of a multi-storeyed building, etc., etc.

This is the author's first book her first novel. For that, it is an excellent book. I bless Smt. Janaki Sriram to write more and more and earn more recognition in society.

It is just a proud moment.

ஈன்ற பொழுதின் பெரிதுவக்கும் தன்மகளைச் சான்றோன் எனக்கேட்ட தந்தை.

12.05.2025

(Dr. K.V. Balasubramanian)

Foreword

Sridevi Srinivasan is the Founder and Director of Little Laudable Learners LLP. A passionate educator, storyteller, trainer, author, and curriculum designer, she is dedicated to nurturing the creativity and communication skills of young minds.

It gives me immense pleasure to write the Foreword for the debut work of Ms. Janaki, Educator at Little Laudable Learners, blogger, writer, and a keen observer of life's little details.

Her maiden book offered me a refreshing perspective — to view a land, an apartment, and the countless lives within it through layers of emotions, everyday moments, and more.

The story begins with suspense, setting an engaging tone right from the start. As a reader, I anticipated a building collapse, an outbreak, or perhaps a crime, but the story cleverly defies all

Foreword

expectations, taking unexpected twists and turns that keep you hooked.

The suspense grips the reader and doesn't let go until the final page.

I loved the author's choice of words in describing the ordinary activities of everyday life. The vivid imagery of the apartment complex, the chaos, the rhythm of life, and the way people communicate within that space is both realistic and poetic.

One line that especially stayed with me was *"The ground will remember..."*, so powerful and profound.

My appreciation to Ms. Janaki for giving life to the ground and to the characters through her words.

I thoroughly enjoyed reading this book. I invite you to immerse yourself in its pages and discover how *the ground remembers*.

I wish this book great success and sincerely hope Ms. Janaki continues to write many more.

Best Wishes
Sridevi Srinivasan
Founder & Director Little Laudable Learners.

Author Note

K B Janaki is a dynamic and versatile writer. Her work spans fiction, non-fiction, poetry, and academic prose. With a deep-seated passion for literature and language. She crafts narratives that explore both the imaginative and the intellectual. Her writing connects readers with diverse experiences and perspectives.

She has contributed articles and poems to *Pine Cone Writing*, *Literary Party*, and the blogs of *Little Laudable Learners* and *Beyond the Box*. Her editorial voice is present in Tamil non-fiction too. One of her early contributions was to the book

Author Note

முக்கனிகளைப் பற்றிய முக்கியமான தகவல்கள், published in 2017.

Janaki holds an M.Phil in English Literature from Chevalier T. Thomas Elizabeth College for Women. Her specialization was in contemporary narratives and cultural criticism.

Her research *Beliefs, Prejudices and Train Journeys: A Study of Select Works by Bishwanath Ghosh*. It reflects her curiosity about travel writing and identity. She has published academic papers in national and international journals such as *Kala: The Journal of Indian Art History Congress* and the anthology *Retelling Indian Myths: An Enquiry*.

Professionally, she wears many hats. She is an educator, proofreader, and content writer. She is actively involved in student enrichment through writing and communication. Her work blends creativity with pedagogy. Her curriculum designs, workshops, and editorial roles reflect a deep commitment to nurturing young minds.

A cancer survivor, she writes with emotional truth and quiet strength. Her experience has deepened her empathy and sharpened her voice. Outside the world of books, she is a passionate film enthusiast. She often explores the intersection of literature and cinema in her creative work and public lectures.

Author Note

When not writing or teaching, she shares her thoughts on janbalan.com and on her YouTube channel @jan_balan, where she speaks about books, language, and life. Her voice is reflective, bold, and empathetic. This book is yet another expression of her belief that language is not just a tool but a journey one that she invites you to travel with her.

Table of Contents

Acknowledgement iv

Foreword vii

Foreword x

Author Note xii

Chapter 1: The Booming City and the Silent Land 16

Chapter 2: Perfect Living, Quiet Cracks 32

Chapter 3: Memories in Hallway 59

Chapter 4: In the Walls 81

Chapter 5: Buried with Intention 90

Chapter 6: Footsteps on Forgotten Soil 103

Chapter 7: Not all the dreams are dreams 109

Chapter 8: The Past That Won't leave 123

Chapter 9: Paper Trails and Ghost Walls 129

Chapter 10: Truth Must Haunt 138

Chapter 11: The Wall that Stayed 155

Chapter 12: Laughter in the cracks 162

Chapter 1: The Booming City and the Silent Land

A soft metallic clang echoed in roads. As the final section of the metro track snapped into place. It was like the release of a breath held far too long. No cheers. The workers just wiped their necks with frayed towels. They passed around a water bottle sticky with cement dust. Somewhere nearby, a plastic flag fluttered limply on a traffic cone. Above, the city shimmered, heat coiling off the pavements like invisible steam snakes.

Selva kept his eyes on the stack of papers, the curve of his pen, the way the nib sometimes caught on the government form's fibrous paper. His signature trembled just slightly on the third copy. Not from doubt. Not quite. His hands were steady for the important parts. Only when it was done stamped, bound, approved did he let his shoulders drop.

He didn't smile. "Everything looks in order," the registrar said. Registrar's eyes scanned the papers with the mechanical gentleness of someone who's done this too many times to be curious. He was a lean man with a parting too straight, the kind that looked drawn with a ruler. "Funny, this plot's been sitting for years. They say some lands are stubborn."

Selva's mouth twitched. "Not stubborn. Just quiet."

The registrar chuckled like it was a joke. "Well, they'll make a complex out of it now. No doubt. Good timing with the metro coming up. Investors are buzzing like flies. Isn't? No doubt. This is the good timing as the metro service is about to finish in few months. The investors would be buzzing like bees.

Selva nodded, not to agree, but to end the conversation. He stood, thumbed the red ink onto the register, the print slightly off-centre like even his body didn't want to leave a trace. A woman at the next table was arguing about a name mismatch. He barely heard her. For a second, a very brief one, his grandfather's voice seemed to flicker in his head:

> *Don't speak of the land. Let the ground keep its own silence. It remembers what we forget.* He pushed the thought away.

As he walked past the rows of rusting metal chairs, Selva didn't look back at the registrar. Outside, the heat had turned the air thick as syrup. He moved toward a waiting grey car. A man leaned against the hood, arms crossed, face unreadable under a dusty cap.

There were no words, just silence, then a nod. Selva lifted the black duffel bag and placed it in the backseat. It wasn't heavy, but it seemed to land with a kind of weight that had nothing to do with mass. The car pulled away, not fast, not slow either, as if speed had consequences.

Selva stood for a moment on the pavement, blinking against the brightness. The city blared on around him autos honking, an ice cream vendor yelling out of tune, a woman shouting into her phone about a bank loan but in his chest, something softened. That was not happiness. That wasn't the shape of it. He knew it, because, there was no sense of satisfaction in heart and mind.

More like the feeling of unclenching a fist you didn't know you'd been holding for years. A long, invisible strain had lived inside him worry, waiting, weariness. He hadn't noticed how tightly he'd been holding on. Until now, when something let go, quiet and deep. It wasn't joy, but a relief. Like a muscle easing after years of silent tension.

He crossed the road without checking for traffic. There behind him, the land now legal, now future-bound waited. Still. Covering a huge, strong life and history.

Not yet. The documents were done. The boundaries marked. But something in him knew the story hadn't begun. Not really. The land waited, like him patient, breathing, heavy with memory. The time to step into that future would come. But not yet.

Chennai used to crawl during the early years of Metro service. People would often comment that the beginning of the Metro wouldn't be this horrible. But regular use of the Metro and sudden rerouting by other transport systems are causing delays.

People planned their weddings around the traff. Auto drivers quoted their rates like astrologers, vague and irrefutable, almost personal. School vans honked like crows squabbling over scraps at 7 a.m. sharp. If you made it to T. Nagar without cursing, you probably weren't from here.

Then came the drills. The barricades, huge lifters and machines. The midnight rumble of steel teeth beneath the roads. For three years, the city lived with one ear tuned to the underground groan of progress. A boy was born in the dust outside a construction site near Saidapet his mother named him Metro. Not short for anything.

When the first train slid out of the tunnel, smooth as a silver snake, it wasn't a ceremony, it was an exhale. A lot of commutes shrank. Cafes opened inside stations. Strangers smiled, once or twice.

A woman met her future husband on the Alandur platform, arguing over who got in line first. They laughed about it later at their wedding reception in Velachery. Even cynics began admitting it: the city had changed.

Real estate didn't just rise, it lunged. Postcards once filled with coconut trees now showed gyms and daycare centres. Schools once brushed aside as "too remote" started trending on parenting blogs. Everyone wanted to live closer to the metro. Even the cow that wandered near the station in Koyambedu. It looked slightly more purposeful.

But one plot stayed untouched. Just behind St. Sebastian's Church. It tucked between a row of half-forgotten rain trees and a shuttered milk booth. The land sat, unbothered, unsold, unspoken. A perfect rectangle, too flat to ignore, too quiet to trust. When prices around it tripled, it didn't budge. Brokers joked it had its own time-zone.

Once it had been something else, a plantain grove, some said. Others remembered it as a garbage site. Some, nothing at all. Memory slipped around it, as if the land itself chose. It stayed. When it finally sold, no ribbon was cut. No press release. Just a silent line of cement trucks arriving one dawn like pilgrims who didn't know what they were praying for.

Story of the Storey

The name they gave it, 'Sunrise Residency', was neither here nor there. Beige walls, angular balconies, a glass-walled gym called Sky Pulse, where no one ever really sweated. The plan was ambitious three towers, each rising fifteen floors into the sky.

Four flats on every floor. A total of 180 homes, drawn and redrawn across dozens of

blueprints until the corners felt too sharp to be lived in. They spoke of natural light, imfloorported tiles, and a meditation deck that pointed vaguely east. On paper, it looked clean. Towers being named "Sapphire, Ruby, and Emerald." It was balanced and real.

First, the wiring wouldn't hold. Engineers rewired the same corridor five times. Then the contractor's phone buzzed with a call from his own number at `02:17` a.m. every night for a week. It Never rang, just buzzed.

Velu, a wiry site worker with more countries under his belt than teeth in his mouth, refused to step into the underground parking after Day 34. He said it smelled "like grief." No one asked him what grief smelled like. He left his helmet by the tea stall. He never collected his final pay.

Ramesh Bhat, the builder, waved it all off. "It's heatstroke," he declared. His arms wide, voice bigger than the site itself. "Even GPS systems go mad in April here. You think people won't?"

He grinned. He always grinned. But one day, during inspection, he stood too long in the lift shaft. After the power cut, when it came back, he just said, "Let's not name this floor 13." There was no argument.

The sun set over the city, casting long shadows across the once-bustling streets that now felt like forgotten passages in a ghost town. The old banyan tree had seen everything births, deaths, festivals, fights. Now, it just drooped, its leaves limp and tired, like it had grown too old for this world. The homes nearby, once alive with voices and laughter, stood quiet. Their walls were starting to fall apart, worn down by time and neglect.

The people who once called this place home were gone now scattered, pushed out by the city's growing hunger for change. It was like the heartbeat of progress had swallowed them without a trace.

Far off, a train whistle cut through the air. It didn't sound hopeful. It sounded hollow. As if it were mourning something that had been left behind something quiet, precious, and gone for good.

It was a city that had forgotten how to mourn its own loss, too caught up in its ambition to notice that it had already lost what mattered most.

In two years in, the tower wasn't quite finished. Only ten floors in two towers are completed. The elevator stalled between floors twice a week, the name board at the gate still read "Sunrise Residency." The security guard's booth didn't have a fan. It just had an old pedestal. It was one plugged into a socket that sparked if you looked at it wrong.

Still, people came. Not all at once, not in a rush. They arrived the way rain

arrives in Chennai, hesitant, uncommitted at first, then suddenly all at once pouring in. Some came with everything packed tight in yellow-lidded cartons. Others brought only a mattress and a temple bell wrapped in old dhotis.

Most were from elsewhere, Pune, Noida, Coimbatore, a few even from Shillong, drawn by glossy promises and looping video tours that never paused long enough on the cracks.

A family on the ninth floor kept the balcony doors shut even in the heat. "Bad breeze," said the grandmother, who tied lemon and green chili garlands on both handles. No one asked what that meant.

Children found each other fast, the way children do. The marble-floored lobby was a siren call echo-rich and parent-proof. They screamed songs, ran races, invented rules.

One little girl, Ruth claimed you could hear a woman laugh and voices from the stairwell. She

Story of the Storey

. Just the brief, sour smell of iron and something like jasmine gone old. Lights didn't flicker. Not every time. Only when you were too tired to really care, or too awake to ignore it. "Software issue," someone said once, without looking up from their phone. Sure. Probably

---

Miles away....

The toe tag read "Unknown Male – 3472/23" in neat, almost apologetic black Sharpie. As if the mortuary assistant had wanted to get that one small thing right. As if that could somehow redeem everything else about the body, which was chaos made flesh.

"He wasn't homeless," Mira said, voice low, deliberate.

She didn't turn from the slab. Her eyes were fixed on what remained of the man if you could call it that. Burned, shrivelled, twisted in places. She stood close enough for the chemical chill of the room to blur against her breath. SI Ravikumar scratched the corner of his chin. Not because it itched. He did that when he didn't want to say something too soon.

"You don't know that," he said finally, keeping his voice even, letting it hang not combative, just gently placing doubt on the table.

Mira exhaled slowly, then stepped a little closer to the corpse. As if proximity could make it speak. "I know his belt had three notches carved in the leather. Notched with a blade. Neatly. Not random. Not with teeth or wire or wear. A knife, deliberate. A tracking system. He marked his weight.

"So?"

"So homeless men don't track their weight. Not like that. Not three notches, evenly spaced, exact angle. That's a habit. That's someone holding on to something, routine, self-worth, memory. Whatever it is, it isn't the behaviour of someone who's given up."

The fluorescent tube above them buzzed gently, the sort of buzz you don't notice unless you already want to leave. The light didn't flicker dramatically like in the movies.

It dimmed and lifted subtly, as if the room itself had lungs, as if it was breathing differently every time you blinked. Ravi didn't like this room. Never had. There was something about the smell, old breath and bleach, but also something under that, like wet gauze forgotten in a drawer.

Too clean in the wrong places, not clean enough in the ones that mattered. The body on the steel table was a study in surrender.

Parts of him were scorched black, coal-coloured and crusted. Other parts, especially around the abdomen, had blistered and bubbled before collapsing. A slow death, if it was death at all. No skin on the hands. Just bone and half-formed tissue.

The fingers were curled inward, not like claws, but like they had tried to hold on. To something or someone or to a secret. The face was gone. Not distorted, absent. Skin peeled back, lips melted away, even the sockets felt too empty, too smooth. You couldn't call it a skull. Not yet. It was more like a suggestion of a face, a shape the fire had begun but not finished.

"You said he had bruises," Mira said, softly now.

As though asking for a truth already known.

"Yeah." Ravi pulled a small notepad from his coat pocket and didn't look at it.

"Upper ribs. Inner arms. Some back trauma. He was grabbed, I think. Maybe held down. Or maybe… maybe he tried to fight someone off before he bolted."

Mira Sen leaned in, not like a detective, not like a scientist and not even like a mourner. She leaned in like someone trying to reconstruct a face from muscle memory, as though the right angle might offer familiarity.

Her eyes moved quickly but not carelessly. Focused, sharp. Except for a small twitch in her cheek that betrayed something, rage maybe, or the ghost of recognition. It came and went.

She crouched, eyes moving from the singed ribcage to the jagged edge of what might once have been a wristwatch. "No fire residue in the lungs."

"You sure?"

"Yes."

She stood again. "That means he was breathing when the fire started. But not during. So either he died before the flames, or"

"Or it wasn't a fire from outside," Ravi finished, frowning.

Mira nodded. She didn't explain further, and Ravi didn't ask. They both stood still for a beat, the silence in the room thick with half-thoughts and possibilities neither of them liked. The cooler behind them hissed briefly and stopped. "He was alive," she said finally. "He ran."

A pause.

"Then he burned."

Ravi blinked, leaned slightly against the steel table as if anchoring himself to its chill.

"And then?"

Her eyes narrowed, not at him, but at something only she could see. Something unspoken, half-formed, running a loop in her head. "Then someone cleaned it up," she said, voice tight. "Too fast. Too clean. Like they were waiting for it."

He didn't respond. There was nothing to say to that, not yet. Just a long, low hum from the tube light. The gentle creak of the doorframe shifting under its own weight. The toe tag fluttered faintly as the morgue's air conditioning kicked in again, whispering across the body like an apology that came too late.

Mira didn't move. Ravi looked at her, and for the first time in a long time, didn't see someone parsing data. He saw someone listening. Not to him. Not to reason. But to the silence of the burned. A silence that said: this isn't over.

Chapter 2: Perfect Living, Quiet Cracks

Nobody ever said they were in Sunrise Residency. The Tower had many places to relax, spend, and gain knowledge. Between the Meditation Dome, the DIY Pottery Deck, the Indoor Planetarium, and the multi-scented Aroma Healing Corridor (yes, really), there was always something going on. At least one event per block, per evening more if Mrs. Alamelu was on the planning committee.

Children had their own kingdom: a soft-floor trampoline arena that pulsed with neon under blacklights, a Minecraft-themed reading room with beanbags shaped like creepers, and a wall painted entirely with chalkboard paint where you could write "I HATE MATHS" in five languages.

Elders attended Tai Chi on the Skywalk, the gym. At dawn, their slow, swaying limbs cut clean silhouettes against the pinkening skyline. Afterward, some lingered for group chanting under the Bodhi ficus. A tree rumoured to have been transplanted from some ancient temple site no one remembered.

Sunrise Residency caters to all ages, not just for the young and energetic. It offers mindful spaces for rejuvenation. Elder residents, like Mrs.

Chitra, often found solace in the Wellness Courtyard. Even the most mundane activities became part of the larger narrative of wellness.

The Wellness Courtyard boasted sound baths on Sundays and "Sun Salutations for the Chronically Tired" on Wednesdays. Couples floated in saltwater pods; divorced men tried gong therapy.

Once, a woman, Mrs Roma from 6A, screamed during a reflexology session. She never came back to the session or to any session. Very soon, she vacated the tower by quoting transfer as the reason.

In the evenings, the Amphitheatre lit up for cinema nights. Hindi classics one-week, Scandinavian noir the next. Teenagers giggled behind columns. Aunties debated the politics of subtitles. One time, someone screened a documentary on medical negligence. It was quietly removed from the schedule after only four viewers showed up, all of them whispering by the end.

Every evening, the tower comes alive with new experiences. There's something for everyone, whether it's the Wellness Courtyard's sound baths or the children's wild adventures in the petting zoo. In between it all, tucked quietly by the elevators, is a little haven for book lovers.

There was a Book Exchange Cabinet that looked like a hobbit door. It nestled beside the elevator lobby, its curved wooden frame and brass knob. It gave it the charm of a portal to another world.

People slipped paperbacks and borrowed thrillers with handwritten notes tucked between pages. Just two floors above, a rooftop café called *Filter & Fiction* buzzed with quiet energy. It was run by three teenage siblings who served strong South Indian filter coffee with literary puns on the menu "Café Kafka" and "Poe-tato Puffs" among the favourites.

Mismatched chairs, fairy lights, and a second-hand poetry shelf made it a sanctuary for the building's dreamers. On the ground floor, tucked behind the parking lot. There was an indoor cricket pitch that witnessed minor wars and lifelong friendships.

Somebody always cheated with an invisible overstep. Somebody always limped away claiming they'd nearly made it to the state team. The pitch echoed with loud appeals and louder laughter. Until the ball inevitably landed in Mrs. Ghosh's balcony and the game paused for diplomacy.

Near the fountain, every second Saturday turned magical for the children in the apartment complex. A mini petting zoo would appear as if out of a storybook, tiny fences were set up, hay scattered, and soft creatures brought in for gentle hands to hold. Children squealed with delight as they fed leafy greens to slow-moving turtles or tried to catch the nimble rabbits that hopped around like fluffy clouds.

Once, to everyone's surprise, there was even a goat named Mani. He had a bell around his neck and a dignified air, walking among the kids as though he were inspecting his estate.

The children adored him instantly, offering him flowers, pebbles, and bits of biscuit. No one knew who brought Mani or where he went after the day ended. He was spoken of for months afterward, part myth, part memory, and entirely magical in their eyes.

Aromatherapy diffusers hissed softly through the corridors. Each block had its own scent. Block A: lemongrass. Block B: sandalwood. Block C: something floral that gave Mrs. Damodaran a headache and eventually forced a residents' vote.

At night, light strips in the floor glowed faintly green. Supposedly bio-sensory, they adjusted based on foot traffic. Sometimes they lit up even when no one was walking. But no one worried on those petty things.

There was just too much to do. Too many events to RSVP[1] to. Too many faces to wave at. No one had time for worry. That is not really. Which is probably why no one noticing the cracks. At least, not yet.

In the midst of all the serenity and well-being, a moment of unexpected disruption found its way in. A chair gave way, a small event that cut through the quiet with a snap. The chair gave way with a snap. Not a loud one.

More like a dry twig being broken very close to the ear clean. It was sudden. For a moment, the Book exchange cabinet froze mid-breath, their eyes wide and fingers still curled around paperback spines and enamel mugs.

It wasn't the peaceful kind of silence they'd been coaxing all morning through guided breathing and *Thich Nhat Hanh* quotes. It was the jolt-before-the-joke kind, brittle and tight.

Mrs. Chitra's folding lawn chair folded a little too literally legs splaying out like they'd finally surrendered. She didn't fall hard. It was more of a controlled collapse.

---

[1] *RSVP – It is a French term mean – "Respond, if you please"*

One of her elbows jutting out, the other flapping for balance, a saree pleat tangled like seaweed around her sandal. She ended up in a sort of side-squat on the grass, blinking behind her rose-tinted reading glasses.

No one laughed right away. Then Kavitha from 9D let out a sputtering snort into her still-steaming turmeric tea. A tension cracked. A few chuckles, half-covered with palms. Someone scrambled to offer a rolled yoga mat. Another dragged over what they grandly called an ottoman.

"Vaanga, vaanga, sit," someone said kindly.

"I'm perfectly fine," Chitra declared.

Smoothing the air around her more than her sari, her smile poised but floating somewhere below the eyes.

"The chair wasn't aligned with my energy field," she added.

It was attempting levity. It landed awkwardly, but no one corrected her.

Up above them, on the eleventh floor not officially handed over yet. But already home to three families and a parrot that mimicked doorbells. An AC unit, newly installed and questionably secured, had begun to drip. A thin stream of water tapped against the lone plantain tree in the Eco Club's rooftop garden. Tap. Tap.

Tap. It sounded almost medical, like IV drip. But no one looked up.

They were too busy rearranging cushions, restacking chairs, brushing grass off their leggings. Life at Sunrise had its hiccups. Better to keep moving. After all, wasn't that what wellness was all about?

Still, when Chitra stood again, brushing invisible dust from her knees, the patch where she'd fallen stayed slightly darker than the rest of the lawn. A damp spot, faintly shaped like a seat, though the sun was strong and there'd been no rain.

The Health Club's sunset jog was underway. It wasn't the most graceful sight. There was more stomping than gliding, more gossip than cardio. Aunts in neon sneakers moved with purpose around the central loop.

They passed the chessboard benches. On the low wall nearby, a row of slippers sat like sleepy pets. The children's park beside them was busy with a strange game. It started off like doctor-patient, then turned into something else entirely.

"I'm the nurse!" shouted little Prabhu.

He had pulled his sock over his head. It looked like a chef's hat that had lost its shape.

"Ghost nurse," corrected Shravan.

His voice serious in that special seven-year-old way. The kids were dragging an old badminton pole, now playing the role of an IV stand.

"She only comes when everything goes too quiet," whispered Malar.

She was the youngest. Her eyes sparkled, but her face was pale with excitement. As "She walks backwards."

Their parents sat nearby, half-listening, half-scrolling. The bench curved beneath them like a tired spine. One mother adjusted her dupatta. Another checked the time but didn't really see it.

"Kanna, what ghost?" asked Prabhu's father. "Did you even finish your shuttle practice?"

He was smiling but clearly not too concerned.

Shravan's mother folded her arms and smiled proudly. "Let them imagine. They're Little Laudable Learners, no? It's in them."

She wasn't wrong.

The school stood a few streets away, behind the old temple tank. It had been started long ago by two sisters Sridevi and Sornapriya. They were scholars, the kind who didn't just teach but built things that lasted.

Today, the campus had story labs, science domes, and students who could speak with confidence in any language. At the entrance, bronze statues of the sisters stood tall. Their arms were folded; eyes fixed ahead. Even the smallest students stood tall too, not just in height but in thought.

The school encouraged them to read, speak, write, and invent their own grammar-filled worlds. One of the sisters' grandsons had even started a book club in the apartment building. Their writing contests, science experiments, and group projects were regularly shared and celebrated.

"You know, right?" said Shravan's mother.

"We live close by. Most of our kids go there. Do check our WhatsApp group, we could send these E-magazine and other coupons."

Prabhu's father nodded. "I just moved here from Kallakurichi. It was my higher official who told me about the school. Is there a college or university nearby too?"

"Yes," she replied. "Right across the avenue. Used to be a women's college years ago. Now it's a university."

She pointed across the road.

"It's called Chevalier T. Thomas Elizabeth University. Recognized by both the state and central government. They have arts, sciences, engineering, and even a department for folk music and heritage crafts."

The campus had its own rhythm. Trees lined the pathways. Old buildings stood side by side with newer ones. Some were named after poets or forgotten queens. Others carried the names of scientists and teachers.

Posters for dance contests and handwritten poetry notices still clung to tree trunks and noticeboards. Students carried notebooks and steel tea flasks. Some rehearsed street plays. Others jotted equations on the backs of old flyers.

The place had grown over the years. But it hadn't lost what made it special. Old banyan trees still shaded the courtyards. You could hear classical music from one room and coding lectures from the next. It was a campus that remembered its past and welcomed new ideas without fuss.

Prabhu listened quietly. He looked around and smiled. The kids had gone back to their grammar game. He felt lucky. This felt like a good place to grow up. Nearby, a couple of older students were hunched over a notebook at the book club. They were working on something. Maybe a story. Maybe a paper. Maybe something else altogether.

And that, too, was part of the magic.

Across the main gate, a faded blue van honked twice, the plumbers had arrived. They moved without ceremony. They had their spanners clinking and green wires snaking down shoulders. They had a long copper pipe that looked unsettlingly like a medical instrument someone had lost a century ago.

Murugesan, the oldest of the crew, pressed his thumb into the space between his eyebrows and glanced up at the building's windows.

Sunrise had its oddities, small, curious things that made the residents pause. Sometimes, the building seemed almost too... perfect. Perhaps that's why, when the workers arrived on-site, the air felt different, as if the place itself had secrets to tell."

"Why do I always feel... off in this place?" he muttered.

"Because you skipped breakfast again, Ayya," the younger one said, nudging him with a laugh. "Heat stroke. Buildings not haunted; your stomach is."

They all laughed, and it echoed between the lobby columns like a group memory being made. Later that night, Murugesan was in a rented room. The single fan there never stopped creaking.

He woke up with a dry ache behind his molars. The smell of old soap lingered in the air, and the scent of burnt linen sat heavy on his tongue. He couldn't name it, and he didn't know when it had started.

Some said Tower C was never completed due to budget cuts. Others whispered it was never meant to be finished at all. Yet every now and then, workers swore they heard footsteps echoing from the direction of that empty plot.

Sometimes, someone called their name, softly, almost kindly, like an old tenant returning to check the taps. Murugesan didn't believe in ghosts. But he'd start carrying vibhuti in his shirt pocket, just in case.

"12A - SHREYA M. – SOFTWARE ENGINEER"

The nameplate was still taped on. It was in Comic Sans, laminated, crooked.

Back inside the tower, as the sun dipped lower, the apartments seemed to develop lives of their own. Shreya's was still settling. Its energy a little off-balance, much like the rest of the tower's hidden layers. Inside, the apartment was still trying to decide if it was a home.

Half-unpacked boxes lined the hallway like shy relatives at a wedding. A plastic bucket stood in for a living room stool. The Pongal in the kitchen was hopeful but lumpy.

Srinidhi stepped in, sunglasses still on. She looked around like she was inspecting something to pull Shreya's leg.

"So, this is the dream, huh?" she said, setting her bag on a box labelled *Bedsheets/Unknown Cables*.

"It will be," said Shreya.

She wielding a ladle and the kind of optimism only EMI-bound people possess. "Pongal first. Then you judge."

A few guests from her office were still loitering in the hall. They were sipping store-brand grape juice and politely complimenting the "airflow." The pooja corner had a new lamp. It is still flickering in fits like it hadn't yet decided if it approved of Shreya. The smell of wet cumin and detergent clung to the walls. Shreya stirred harder.

Srinidhi perched on the kitchen slab, cross-legged like a cynical crow. "I'm telling you," She said, licking the condensation from her mug, "my gut is twitching. This place is too, symmetrical. I feel there would be a story of the Storey,"

Shreya didn't look up. "What does that even mean?"

"It means, I don't trust spaces where nothing is out of place. You ever notice the walls here don't echo?"

"They do," said Shreya, "when mantras were chanted during Pooja, we could hear."

"No, not that kind. Not real echo. Emotional echo." Srinidhi swung her legs down. "Some buildings remember things. This one feel like it's trying too hard to forget." She paused.

Shreya's eyes landed on a faint smudge beneath the living room switchboard. Not a stain, more like a fingerprint made in reverse. A clean patch in the shape of a square, like something had been removed. Recently. Carefully.

"Hmm," she muttered.

"What?"

"Nothing," Srinidhi said

But her gaze lingered. Shreya sighed, scraping the pot. "Please go write that into your blog. "I don't write crime novels."

"Exactly."

5B   In Flat 5B of Sunrise Residency, seventeen-year-old Varun leaned over the bathroom sink one humid Thursday evening, toothbrush in hand, lazily swirling it through a pool of minty foam. His school shirt was half-buttoned, collar still damp from his rushed shower, and the bathroom light buzzed above him with its usual dying-fly flicker. He looked up.

For a split second, so fast it might have been a blink gone rogue, his reflection wasn't there at the mirror. Instead, he saw a cracked tile floor. Not his bathroom's pinkish tiles, but grey ones, cold and institutional-looking.

A green curtain hung to one side. It was fabric but that brittle, clinic or hospital-plastic kind that always smelled like sanitizer. Right in the middle of the room: an empty metal cot with rust blooming around the hinges like disease. No sound. No movement. Just that.

Varun stumbled back, his toothbrush clattering into the sink. When he looked again, the mirror showed only himself. A wide eyes, suds on his chin, the faint acne shadow he hated. He didn't scream. Not immediately. He stood still, barely breathing, heart ticking hard in his ears. Then he ran out and told his mother.

She panicked the way middle-class mothers of only son's panic. Not yelling, but organizing. Within 24 hours, Varun had an appointment at the *Sun & Sage Wellness Centre*, located above the Karunya Supermarket, beside a failing Pilates studio and a store that sold only Himalayan pink salt lamps.

The therapist, young, kind, and named Deepika, had soft eyes and softer sentences. "You've probably experienced what we call retinal memory trauma," she said. Scribbling it down as if naming it reduced its power. "Sometimes, the mind replays a sensory snapshot from a past moment. Like déjà vu. But visual. Detached from context."

It sounded scientific comforting and a smart way to reduce fear. Varun nodded, grateful for the phrase. It made everything easier to file away. Still, when he got home, he avoided mirrors. He brushed his teeth by memory, head tilted away, eyes half-closed. He even stopped using his front camera unless it was for class.

For two whole weeks, he lived in a reflection-free bubble. He shaved badly. Missed a strand of toothpaste on his lip one morning that earned a teasing jab from his neighbour, Aakash. Once, he walked past a shop window and ducked before he could glimpse himself.

At school, no one knew. He still cracked jokes during history. He cursed the Wifi like everyone else. But every now and then, when the tube light flickered or a metal chair scraped the floor just wrong, a cold knot formed in his chest.

Varun didn't know what was worse, that he might have imagined it... or that he hadn't. Somewhere deep inside, in a corner of the brain no therapy could sweep clean, Varun suspected the mirror hadn't shown him a memory. It had shown him a place. Maybe, just maybe. That place had looked back.

It arrived quietly, as these things usually do, wedged in the Sunrise Residency WhatsApp group between a Swiggy coupon code offering 25% off biryani and a blurry photo of someone's cat on a scooter.

"THE LAND WHERE TIME STOPPED: Forgotten Institutions of the City."

That was the headline. The link led to a blog, run by someone with the handle @historymorphosis. The kind of blog you'd usually skim through at midnight and forget by morning.

It had all the ingredients: misty nostalgia, sepia filters, paragraphs beginning with "Little did they know..." The writing teetered between romantic ramble and shaky research. But it was the photos that gave people pause.

One, in particular. A grainy photograph, probably taken in the '80s, showed a single-storey building, low, squat, with a tiled roof and slatted windows half-covered by creepers. The signage was bleached by time. It was not decodable.

Nobody said it aloud, but everyone did the same thing. They zoomed in. They searched for something familiar, something they recognized. What they found was surprising. At the far edge of the building, behind a tangle of bougainvillea and a rusted-out van, was a gate. But not just any gate.

It looked exactly like theirs. Or rather, the gate that used to be here, before the land was flattened, the soil churned, and Sunrise Residency rose in its place like a concrete rebirth. Same curved ironwork. Same flaking white paint. Even the old banyan roots that curled nearby like sleeping snakes.

The silence in the group chat lasted a full four hours, which was practically geological time in WhatsApp terms. Then someone, Arun from 6A, the admin and self-appointed conspiracy slayer, typed: **"Fake news. Don't forward these things."**

But he didn't delete it. No one did. It sat there in the chat like a shadow no one wanted to touch. Not unread, not read, just present, like a lump beneath the digital mattress. The kind that kept the screen buzzing at odd hours, even when all notifications were off.

Later that evening, Mrs. Lakshmi from 8C messaged privately asking if anyone remembered what the land was before the apartments. "I think there were sheds?" she wrote. "Or was it an orphanage?"

No one replied. But many forwarded the message. Shreya forwarded it to Srinidhi. Srinidhi, in turn, replied, "It wasn't an orphanage. I've seen that gate before." That single sentence unsettled more people than the article itself.

Everyone knew Srinidhi wasn't the type to gossip or imagine things. She worked in law enforcement, some said. A private investigator, others whispered. She had this way of listening too closely and noticing too much.

Now she'd noticed... that.

The forwarded post was never discussed again in public. But over the next week, more curtains stayed closed during the day. Children stopped playing near the north wall where the bougainvillea grew too wild.

One morning, someone found a folded printout of the blog tucked into the building's notice board, pinned with a rusted hospital tag. No one claimed it.

5B Outside Flat 5B, the corridor held its usual early evening hush, the kind that came just before dinner smells and the clatter of pressure cookers. Somewhere down the hall, a TV played a devotional song, faint and fluttering like a half-remembered dream.

A sudden breeze slipped through the slightly open stairwell door. Just a thread of air, not even enough to lift a saree pallu. It was just enough to stir the paper rangoli resting near the lift. It had been placed there that morning, hand-cut, bright with turmeric yellow and hibiscus red, a small token of festive spirit taped carefully to the tiles.

Now, the wind found it. The paper lifted. Not violently. Not even quickly. It rose in a gentle arc, like it had somewhere specific to be. Then, mid-air, it paused, as if listening, before slowly folding itself inwards. One corner tucked in. Then the next. Silent, precise. Fold after fold, like an invisible hand was teaching it to vanish.

It hovered for just a second longer. Then dropped, without fanfare, straight into the open mouth of the garbage chute. Gone. No one saw it happen. There were no footsteps in the corridor. No phones lifted to record. No bored security guard glancing up from his chair.

Nothing. Just a paper rangoli that disappeared, crease by mysterious crease.

3C

Later that night, Mrs. Shobana from 3C would swear she heard rustling sounds near the garbage chute when she went out to dump kitchen waste. She'd describe it as "like someone folding laundry in the dark."

But she'd laugh it off. She always did. Because strange things only happened in movies and in WhatsApp forwards. Certainly not in Sunrise Residency. Not this time.

Mira and SI Ravi sat on the hood of his Bolero, the old one with one cracked headlight and a glovebox full of case files no one had ever digitized. It smelled faintly of burnt clutch and ghosted passengers, the kind of passengers who never slammed the door, never adjusted the rearview mirror, never asked to stop for water.

The tea in their paper cups was lukewarm by now. The kind of lukewarm that tasted like the day had tried, but ultimately decided it wasn't worth the effort.

"I shouldn't have called you," Ravi said. His voice wasn't an apology. It was softer than that. Not regret, just the sound of someone naming a truth that had been sitting between them, legs crossed, watching.

"You're right," Mira said.

She took a sip, but the cup had collapsed slightly at the rim, and the tea pooled at the edge of her lower lip before sliding down unnoticed.

"But you did," she added, wiping her chin with the back of her sleeve.

He looked at her. Really looked. But she didn't meet it. Her eyes were elsewhere locked on a rusted lamppost where a single crow had landed and stared back at her like it owned the deed to the street.

"You know," Ravi started.

He drawing the sentence out like he wasn't sure if it wanted to be born, "the last time I saw burns like that... it was a lab fire."

He waited, half expecting her to interrupt. She didn't. "Even then," he continued, "there was a pattern. A source. A point of ignition. Here? It's like..." He searched for the word. Couldn't find it. Settled instead on what it felt like. "...Like the fire came from memory."

Mira didn't respond. Her thumb moved along the paper rim of the cup, slow and methodical. She was trying to trace a map only she could see. Her mind was somewhere else entirely, looping through burn patterns, failed autopsies, the way the lungs had been clean, too clean.

Heat from the inside.

What does that?

Fever. Radiation. Rage.

Or maybe...

Maybe some buildings don't like what walks in. Maybe they burn it out like infection. Maybe Velu didn't die in a fire maybe he was rejected. "I ran the duffel bag number," she said. Her voice was flat, but her hand gripped the cup tighter than before.

"It's Velu."

Ravi frowned. "Velu?"

She nodded. "Site worker. Migrant. Quiet. Used to send money to a dialysis center in Madurai. For his mother. Slept on the site itself sometimes. Too many loans. Bad loans. The kind with men behind them."

"They beat him up?"

"Last week. Near the drainage canal."

"He lived through that?"

"Yeah."

"But not this?" She didn't answer.

The crow shifted its feet. Ravi took a breath and let it out in pieces. "They're moving the case," he said. "To Central."

Mira raised an eyebrow but didn't speak. "They said it's an electrical thing. Some old transformer blew. Maybe the guy got caught in the arc."

"Transformer didn't leave bruises."

"I know."

"Did they even do a blood test on the body?"

"They didn't have to. The lab's... backed up."

"Of course, it is," she muttered. Then added, after a beat, "They want it closed."

"Of course, they do."

Silence again, but this time it wasn't shared. It was side-by-side, like strangers waiting for separate buses. She sipped her tea again, more for the ritual than the taste. The cup gave a little more. The cardboard, now soft, dented under her grip like it wanted to disappear.

"You still remember Arumugam's case?" Ravi asked suddenly.

She smiled faintly. "The school teacher with the missing toe and the haunted well?"

He nodded.

"They shut that too," she said.

"They always shut the good ones."

"That one wasn't good."

"It was messy. That's why it was good."

She didn't argue.

A scooter passed behind them, the driver humming something tuneless. A woman on the pillion held a bag of greens and looked directly at Mira as they went by, as if trying to place her face. Then gone.

"How you conclude to Velu?" Ravi questioned.

"I remember his belt tag, didn't we catch hold of him when we are finding evidence in Arumugam's case? A crazy dollar with the story of Mother in it."

Ravi checked his phone for the image, he found there was a dollar in the belt of the dead person.

"How would this one evidence will help to circle it back to him?"

"I have pulled some strings to search the person. If he is alive, he is not. If we cannot find him. He will be the dead."

"You think Velu knew something?" Ravi asked.

"I think he felt something. Maybe not with words. But with his bones."

Ravi leaned back onto his elbows. "I hate that feeling. When someone dies not because they were in the wrong place, but because they realized what place they were in."

Mira nodded slowly. Then, as if to herself: "There's a difference between being lost and being erased."

"You think he was erased?"

"No," she said. "I think he left a trace. They just don't want us to know where to look."

The crow flew away suddenly, wings slicing through the air like scissors. Ravi stood first. Tossed his empty cup into the municipal bin across the road.

"They told me not to involve you," he said.

Ravi brushing his hands together like dust had accumulated from the conversation.

"I figured."

"I didn't listen."

She smiled. But not at him. He paused. "Be careful, Mira. This one's... thin. The walls aren't thick enough to separate what happened from what's still happening."

"I know."

"I'm serious."

"I know," she said again.

But the way she said it sounded like: *But I'm already inside it.* She tossed her cup. Made it. The hollow thud was the only clean thing about the day. He walked back to the Bolero. She stood behind, watching the road curve away. The city breathed somewhere behind the heat haze. Before getting in, Ravi turned once more.

"You'll write about it, won't you?"

"I already did."

He didn't ask where. He didn't need to. He knew it would be somewhere anonymous, somewhere careful, somewhere that would disappear if you searched too hard.

"Title?"

She looked down the road and whispered, not for him, maybe not even for herself. *"Burn Pattern."* He nodded. Drove away. No goodbye. Just taillights, pulsing once, then swallowed by the bend. She didn't move for a long time. Just listened to the silence the city made when it didn't know it was being watched.

Chapter 3: Memories in Hallway

"They've changed the vaccine," whispered Mr. Rajagopal.

He was staring at the ceiling fan, unblinking. As though it might detach and slice him clean through the middle. His voice wasn't loud. It didn't need to be. The words seeped through the flat like moisture.

No one knew who heard his whisper about vaccine or his words "tap, tap"?

First maybe his wife, bringing in the drying clothes, or maybe their neighbour Mrs. Leela. She paused mid-pickle-making when she saw him out on the balcony, wrapped in a wool shawl, mumbling at the sun.

He hadn't left the balcony in two days. Heat shimmered off the tiles like oil in a pan. Still. he sat there, knees drawn to his chest, tapping the railing in steady sets of three. Tap. Tap. Tap. Pause. Tap. Tap. Tap. No one remembered him doing that before.

"Was he always like that?" someone in the family group chat typed.

His son said no. Not always. It started after the power cut. That Friday evening, just after dinnertime, the entire Ruby block had blacked out for eleven minutes and twenty-three seconds. The residents of Flat 10C lit a candle.

The younger daughter laughed nervously and made shadow puppets. But the old man just stood in the dark kitchen, unmoving, hand pressed against the microwave door.

After the lights returned, he began tapping on the table, on the balcony rail and on his own thigh. There were three short taps and a pause.

At first, it felt harmless. Maybe even charming. An old man's new quirk. But then he started saying things. "They've hidden it in our bones. The leftover batch. From 2020."

"Appa, what batch?"

But he wouldn't answer. He'd just rock back and forth slightly. Like, he was measuring the weight of something unbearable.

"There were sirens," he murmured.

"Too many sirens. They wrapped them in plastic, like grocery items. But this this sickness it's slower. More patient. It waits in your marrow."

His granddaughter, Amudha, eleven and recently promoted to official family peacemaker, tried her best. She showed him old temple elephant reels on YouTube. He used to love those. But when she held the phone up, he swatted it away with surprising strength.

"The screen is watching me!" he hissed.

The phone skidded across the floor. His wife didn't speak for the rest of the evening. By the next day, neighbours had begun to whisper. Mrs. Leela again her voice soft but urgent. "He's tapping in his sleep now. I could hear it through the wall. Three taps. Always three."

In the kitchen, his son whispered to his wife.

"He was normal till last week. Really. Ever since the blackout... and that smell."

"What smell?"

"The garbage chute. Burnt bandages. Like a hospital. Like chemicals."

"Maybe he's remembering the lockdown?"

"Maybe." But he didn't sound sure.

They tried to bring him inside. His daughter offered him buttermilk, cold and frothy. He refused. His wife said she dreamt of him pressing his palm against her forehead, over and over, as if checking for fever. But in the dream, his palm left a mark. An imprint of something not quite human.

No one said these things out loud. They texted them. They forwarded memes and Swiggy codes to distract themselves.

By evening, Mr. Rajagopal had stopped speaking entirely. Instead, he stripped to his veshti, dipped his fingers in leftover sambar, and began writing on the living room wall. Not words equations. Frantic loops and angles. Arrows pointing to nowhere. The curry dripped down in orange trails.

His grandson tried to take a photo, but the image wouldn't save. The phone glitched, vibrated for five seconds, then restarted. When it came back on, the wallpaper had changed. He remembers the image from somewhere. So, he frantically scrolled through his WhatsApp. It was the image from the blog everyone shared before in the group "**THE LAND WHERE TIME STOPPED.**" No one knew where it had come from.

Someone finally called the ambulance. They came quietly, with no siren. As if the building had been flagged. "Don't let them take me back to surgery!" Mr. Rajagopal screamed. "I have all my organs this time!"

He thrashed as they strapped him down. The shawl fell away, revealing lines drawn in sambar across his chest diagrams of lungs, arteries, a liver rendered like a school biology chart. He had drawn incisions on himself, marked with tiny x's.

"Tell them," He pleaded, his eyes wild. "Tell them I remember the hallway. The nurse with no eyes. The clipboard. She said I wasn't finished. They said it wasn't my time yet. But they tagged me. I saw my own tag. I saw"

They closed the ambulance doors before he could finish. That night, his granddaughter lay awake, replaying the sound of his tapping. Tap. Tap. Tap. Pause. She blinked at the ceiling, and for a moment, just one flicker of a moment, she thought she saw him standing near the window.

But it wasn't the grandfather she knew, it was a thinner version, almost translucent, hands clasped behind his back like a surgeon about to step into theatre. She rubbed her eyes. Gone. That night, the apartment was quiet. Not peaceful just stunned into stillness, the way a house feels after an argument no one won.

Someone had cleaned the sambar from the walls. There was faint orange streaks left in the grout lines, and the smell of tamarind clung to the curtains. No one mentioned the tapping anymore. But everyone heard it, faintly, like a memory repeating itself down the hallway.

At 3:12 a.m., the phone rang. It was the hospital. Flat 10C never knew exactly what they said. Only that Mr. Rajagopal from 10B had stopped breathing sometime after midnight. No heart attack. No fever. No diagnosed condition. The doctor used a phrase that stuck in the granddaughter's mind like a thorn: *"His body let go, but not all at once."*

The family didn't hold a proper cremation. Not right away. The body had to be "observed." That was the word the hospital used observed, like he was still being studied. Or perhaps still studying something himself.

The official cause of death read: **Acute neurocognitive failure with dissociative behaviour.** The report looked official. Sterile. Boring. But his son couldn't bring himself to delete the old man's last voicemail, a message sent by mistake. All it said was:

> "I've remembered something I shouldn't have. The power didn't go out. The building did."

After the rites, Amudha found herself sitting in his balcony chair. His wool shawl still hanging on the backrest. From that spot, you could see the garbage chute. The microwave door reflected sunlight. From somewhere inside the flat though she'd never find out where came a faint sound.

Story of the Storey

Tap, Tap, Tap, Pause and nothing else. Just the ceiling fan turning slowly overhead.

9B It began quietly, the way nightmares usually do. Mrs. Anjali from was not the type people noticed unless she was missing. She walked like her feet were apologizing for touching the ground. She wore socks even in summer. She always kept a roll of eucalyptus balm in every bag. It was the way she turned it in her fingers over and over, cap off, cap on that people remembered, if they remembered anything at all. One day she fell.

Her mannerism had a point of origin. A month after, there was a blackout. One of those odd ones: only Ruby tower went dark. Though the others glowed steady like nothing had happened.

Anjali had been in the elevator alone, descending from the terrace. It stopped between floors. The lights were out and fan was dead. Her voice never loud to begin with bounced around the metal box like a trapped bird.

When the power returned five minutes later, the CCTV caught her stumbling out. She has eucalyptus roll in hand and twisting the cap open and shut-in frantic repetition. Her mother found her kneeling in the living room, nose bleeding slightly. Her eyes fixed on the microwave, whispering, "It's full of teeth."

After that elevator, the balm rolls never left her hand. Even in school, even while eating. She never explained. Just kept turning it, as though some hinge in her mind had come loose. She was trying to screw it back in place.

The first time she sleepwalked, her father found her at 3 a.m.. She was neatly rearranging her shoe rack by colour and left-right orientation. She was humming. Not a song he recognized. But her fingers moved precisely, like following old blueprints.

The second time, she stood under the corridor tube light, facing the elevator doors. She was humming again. This time, her mother recognized the tune: a Tamil lullaby. But, she hadn't sung since Anjali was a toddler. When her mother called out, Anjali didn't flinch. She didn't blink. Just said, softly, "They made me lie down."

The third time, she was seen by the domestic help from 8C. The woman had come out to shake a mop cloth dry when she looked up and saw the girl standing on the parapet, arms stretched to either side, as if bracing for some invisible procedure.

"They're calling me to surgery," Anjali whispered, almost kindly.

What happened next was not a fall. Not in the way gravity understands it. It was sudden, chaotic, with flailing limbs and last-minute regret. There was no stumble to blame, no gust of wind to push, no scream to mark the moment. Just a slow, eerie motion. As if her body had simply decided it no longer belonged to the world it stood on.

It left the parapet not with violence, but with something stranger, purpose. Like a note leaving the mouth of a singer. Effortless, yet driven by breath, by will, by something unseeable and deep inside. Freely, yes. But also, as though called by something old, and final. It was not quite explainable.

The scream came five seconds later from her mother. She had been in the bathroom, pouring boiling water into a bucket. She was unaware her daughter had just stepped into air. What the domestic help said afterward changed with each retelling.

Some said Anjali looked serene. Others said her body twisted mid-air, resisting descent. A few whispered that her fall wasn't vertical at all. She drifted, momentarily, toward the building opposite, arms raised like she was reaching for gloved hands behind a glass.

The ambulance came. Took longer than it should have. The driver's eyes were red. He said nothing. Didn't ask for directions. Just looked up once at the 9th floor. He shook his head slowly, and drove off with her body. It was still warm and could sense the still smelling of eucalyptus. The police ruled it a suicide. Open-and-shut case, it was too neat.

No one wanted to mention the tube lights that had started to flicker in that corridor. Or that, at exactly the time she fell, the elevator opened on its own and stayed open until sunrise. Her mother stopped using the microwave. The eucalyptus balm was found in the garden hedge. Cap still on.

It began with the blackout. A three-hour blackout on a muggy Tuesday evening, written off as EB maintenance. When the lights flickered back on, something no one could name it, but everyone felt it had shifted.

4D The pets were the first to vanish. Kumudha from 4D found her parakeet. It was staring at a corner of the living room wall for ten minutes straight. It was a vivid green bird. It was known to squawk movie dialogues and curse words. But now eerily silent.

Then, without warning, it took off straight into the switchboard with a crack. When she opened the panel, expecting feathers or blood, there was nothing. Just an empty nest of wires, and the faint smell of antiseptic.

7A   In 7A, the neighbour's ginger cat, usually aloof and judgmental. It started rubbing itself feverishly against cold appliances fridge, washing machine, even the microwave.

On Thursday, it slipped into the laundry room. The door never closed, and there were no windows. But it never came out. They even shook the detergent box. Nothing.

Next came the ants. A clean line, black as stitching thread, marching out from beneath the fridge in 3C. The residents watched, frozen. The ants didn't scatter when someone stamped nearby.

They moved with ceremony. They made a spiral on the kitchen tiles perfect and mathematical. Then, as if a silent order had been given, they stopped moving. Every single one. Dead.

Then, the boy. Vishwa was six. He had three missing front teeth and a talent for hiding in impossible spaces. The day he vanished, it had rained just a drizzle, warm and soft. The kids in the building played hide and seek on the fifth-floor landing.

Vishwa was "It." Then he wasn't. His friends said they heard him giggling near the trash chute. "He's hiding behind it," one girl offered, hopeful. But when they looked, there was only a faint smell of turmeric and metal.

The building went into emergency mode. Ducts were opened; sump tanks were drained. Security guards were asked. Then accused, then asked again. Flyers were printed and then removed within days, too painful to look at.

His mother, Ambika, never stopped searching. She slept with her shoes on, one foot half off the bed, the way Vishwa used to sleep. She kept the fridge light on every night. "He hates the dark," she repeated, almost conversationally, while folding his clothes.

During the investigation, police found Vishwa's drawing note. Filled with images. When they inquired, parents informed, he has not seen these things in his life time. But the case stays open as 'kidnap.'

By the weekend, other things began to happen. It is like small, unnerving things. Kumudha from 4D developed a habit of touching all her door handles three times before entering or exiting a room.

4D

Story of the Storey

"Don't know why," she said. "Just feels wrong otherwise."

Her eyes darted when she said it, like she was expecting someone to correct her.

Mohan from 2B started whistling constantly tuneless. It was an anxious burst. When asked, he blinked and said, "I don't whistle." His wife had recorded him one night, pacing their kitchen, the sound almost like something echoing.

Even the walls began to behave strangely. Paint began to peel in long. Almost deliberate strips, curling inward like they were hiding something. A stain shaped like a surgical mask appeared under the stairs. The building supervisor painted over it. It came back.

Residents whispered about a hum a soft. It is electrical buzz that seemed to travel from room to room. But it wasn't tied to any device. It came mostly at night. Some said it sounded like an old hospital monitor. Others said it resembled breathing.

Still, the power would cut. Short bursts this time five minutes, seven minutes, rarely more. But always at odd hours. 2:03 a.m. 4:47 a.m. Once, 11:11 p.m. which made the WhatsApp group unreasonably superstitious for a whole day.

After one such flicker, Meenakshi from 6C woke up to find her bathroom mirror fogged over though she hadn't used it. On the glass, drawn by an invisible finger, were three perfect circles, one inside the other.

She cleaned it. It came back.

In the lift, the floor buttons stopped lighting up correctly. People began stepping in, pressing 4, only to arrive at 7. They'd find themselves alone between floors. They stare at the numbers flickering nonsensically, 2, 5, 9, 3, 1, 6. Then a blackout.

The building's maintenance head, a chain-smoking man named Nagaraj. He claimed it was nothing but loose wiring. "You'll hear ghosts if you want to," he said. Tapping his spanner like it was a magic wand. But after his own tools vanished mid-repair, he stopped answering calls after dusk.

Still, no one could explain the dreams. Residents reported them like weather reports: I had it again last night. The hallway one. Or: This time I was strapped down. It smelled like Dettol.

In nearly every dream, there was a corridor. Either it is too white or too clean. With echoing footsteps and distant beeping. Some said they saw a hand reach for them. Some say it is gloved and cold.

Others woke up screaming after being rolled into an elevator with no doors. Just an opening that led downward, forever.

Even the soundscape of the building had changed. The wind through the stairwell had taken on a wheeze. The garbage chute made a clanking, wet sound, like someone stirring soup. A laugh, faint and childlike, sometimes echoed across the fifth-floor landing. No one checked anymore.

Then came the mail. Old envelopes with no return addresses. Slipped under doors in the early hours. Each held just one thing: a thin, official-looking slip of paper stamped, creased, oddly cold with a name, often theirs, followed by a single word.

"DISCHARGED."

2A It began with Sharada from 2A. At first, she kept the dreams to herself. She thought they were just strange remnants of a late dinner or her migraine tablets. But when they began to repeat, each night more vivid than the last. She mentioned them to her husband in a tentative whisper. Naming them aloud might give them permission to stay.

"I'm in a room," she said.

"White tiles. Not grimy, not horror-movie dirty. Just sterile. Too clean. It smells like Dettol. There's always a nurse with too many fingers handing me a clipboard. The language on it isn't Tamil, isn't English, but I can read it perfectly. Like I always knew it."

Her husband had chuckled. "Maybe you've got some secret past life in Switzerland." She didn't laugh. "There's a man crying in the next bed.

Every night. I never see his face, but I know he's missing something." Then there was the dripping. A soft, wet pat... pat... pat.

As if something viscous was leaking behind the walls. Her husband brushed it off with a gas leak joke. Until the dreams found him too. Same pale room. Same silent nurse. Same clipboard laid just so. Always, that same faint, metallic scent clinging to the air like memory.

By the third night, both Sharada and her husband stopped sleeping with the lights off. She took to double-knotting her nightgown's drawstrings. He wore his wristwatch to bed, though it left a red mark. They started keeping a flask of coffee ready on the bedside table, in case they woke up in cold sweat. Which they did.

More troubling, though, was how real the dreams felt. These weren't the blurry, half-melted images of subconscious clutter. These dreams had memory, more texture and a lot of mental weight.

6C "You could smell them when you woke up," Sharada said to Meenakshi from 6C one morning. "Like hospital soap, iron. Like blood. You can taste it in your teeth."

Her voice had developed a new habit. She cleared her throat twice before saying anything. A small double-cough. People began to notice. Her students at the tuition centre started mimicking her unconsciously.

At home, her husband flinched whenever she did it, as though it signaled something was about to change again. It wasn't just her. Others in the building began to talk.

Nagaraj, the grizzled supervisor, had dreamt of an elevator with no walls. It was just tiled panels and a small button labeled only "AGAIN." He said he pressed it. He said, "He felt the descent. Later, he woke up with bruises on both palms."

5B Kamini from 5B had started sleep-speaking. Her husband recorded her one night. She was reciting words. When they run through an audio spectrogram, the cadence resembled Sanskrit chants played backward.

More residents were whispering about "the room." The sterile one. The nurse. The clipboard. Some said the dripping had changed from water to something thicker. May be oil, blood, or milk. Everyone described it differently, but all agreed on the sound: pat... pat... pat.

Sharada started visiting her General Physician. He is kind, baffled man who checked her blood pressure thrice in a row. He told her everything was "normal, but unusual." When she left, he rubbed Dettol on his hands a second time. Not because she was unclear, but because he felt watched.

Meanwhile, her husband had developed a mannerism of his own: he started checking door handles. Constantly. Even after locking one, he'd press it, pull it, test it three times. Once, Sharada asked if he was okay.

"Just making sure I'm not back in there," he muttered, and didn't explain further.

At some point, no one remembers when, it became taboo to explain the place which their dream land. Instead, people replaced it with "the place," or "that room."

As if the name itself was a summoning. Some people began wearing surgical masks indoors again. That was not because of a virus, but to keep the dreams out. They believed the air itself had memory.

Even the children stopped playing "doctor" in the corridors. The toy stethoscopes vanished. The junior nurse costume in the playroom disappeared. No one noticed, or at least, no one admitted they had.

One night, Sharada dreamed of something new. This time, the nurse leaned close, her fingers long and webbed. Her voice a perfect blend of her mother's and her school Principal's, and whispered, "You've already signed. The next one is for consent."

Sharada looked down. She was holding the clipboard again. The letters on the page were shifting. Yet she could read every word. She understood.

When she woke up, there were smudges of ink on her fingers. Her husband didn't dream that night. He only stared at the ceiling for hours, He was whispering numbers, serial codes, perhaps, or IDs. At 3:17 a.m., he sat up and said, "There's no floor under our bed. Just tile."

The next morning, they removed all the mirrors from their house. They stopped opening the fridge unless absolutely necessary. They unplugged the microwave. Sharada, always the morning puja kind of woman, stopped lighting agarbattis. She said the smoke reminded her of cauterization.

The new security guard in the building. A wiry teenager as a security with headphones always in one ear. He complained that the CCTV footage kept going blank around 2:45 a.m. "Just static or white. Sometimes I think I see a mask." He laughed, but it didn't reach his eyes.

The dreams spread like fever. People talked less in elevators. No one stood near the trash chute. A few flats installed second locks. Some stopped sleeping entirely. Then came the notices. Thin envelopes slipped under doors. Each contained a single paper, smelling faintly of ethanol. On it was a message typed in grayscale:

"SURGERY COMPLETE. PLEASE WAIT FOR TRANSFER."

Sharada didn't scream when she read hers. She simply folded it once, then again, then once more. She placed it inside a stainless steel dabba meant for pickles. She locked it.

Every night now, before bed, she touches all four corners of the kitchen counter twice. Then coughs, twice. Then says, "I'm awake, I'm awake," three times. She hasn't dreamt in two weeks. But she still wakes up with that smell in her throat.

Sometimes, when she passes the mirror in the hallway, her reflection coughs before she does.

The report was filed. SI Ravi signed it with a pen. It looked like it had survived a nervous breakdown. It has bitten through at the cap, chewed down to the plastic. The ink dragged slightly across the paper like it didn't want to be there.

"Accidental death due to chemical combustion."

That was the line. Plain and clinical, as if carefully drained of emotion. It sat there on the page, stripped of any warmth or weight, dehydrated of truth. He stared at the words, willing them to shift, to reveal something beneath their stillness.

As if, if he looked long enough. They might sprout something foul, fungus. It is blooming in the folds of denial. That mould creeping through the corners of certainty or worse, something quieter. Something that didn't smell or grow, but simply stayed. Like guilt, settling in before it had a name.

Across the room, Mira stood by the window. Her hands were folded, but not in a peaceful way. Just two fists trying not to make a decision. A pigeon tried to land on the rusted ledge outside, flapped twice, gave up, and disappeared into the dense, sunless slice of morning.

"You're not going to let this go," Ravi said.

Ravi didn't phrase it as a question. Because it wasn't. She didn't answer. At least not immediately. There was no flare of righteousness, no call to arms. Just silence, long and slow, like water finding the deepest part of the room.

"As I said, I already wrote about it," she said, her voice a little frayed at the edges. "No names. Just... questions." Ravi exhaled, pushed his chair back slightly. "Your blog?"

She nodded. His eyes narrowed, not with suspicion, but recognition. She didn't have to say which blog. He'd read it, more than once, under a fake name on a shared laptop in the station break room.

"What did you call it?"

Mira smiled, but it barely touched her mouth. It wasn't the kind of smile you give someone. It was the kind you keep for yourself. Like a bruise you check in the mirror.

"I will continue to write about this under the same title, *Burn Pattern.*"

Mira said it like it was already out there in the world, already living its own strange life, already read by people who didn't know they needed to read it.

Chapter 4: In the Walls

That night, the post sat quietly on Mira's blog. There was no tags and no flashy headlines. Just a plain title and a threadbare paragraph. It was enough to raise eyebrows, not enough to raise alarms. She didn't expect responses. Not right away.

So, when the comment appeared three hours later, it felt like a tap on the shoulder in a locked room. There was no username, no timestamp, and even the IP was not traceable. It was just a line, plain and precise:

> **"You don't know where he was before the road. That ground still remembers a lot of things. Stay away from the vents."**

Mira stared at it. Once, or maybe twice. By the fifth reading, her hand was hovering near the screen, not to touch, just to check if it was really there. The monitor flickered once, briefly. A flutter, like a pulse caught in the throat. Then it settled. Still. Silent. Complicit.

She didn't delete the comment. She didn't reply either. She just leaned back in her chair. Let the dark edge of the screen reflect in her eyes. She didn't sleep that night. Not out of fear. Fear would have been easier. It has rules. It rings alarms. It gives you options: run, hide, fight.

This was different. This was a kind of knowing. A knowing she had no language for. The kind that arrives as a smell before a memory. The kind that sits in your lungs long after the smoke has left the room.

This wasn't new. She'd seen it before. Cases shelved too early. Names buried before questions. Warnings wrapped in politeness, in caution, in budgets.

But this time it wasn't just a person they were trying to forget. It was a place. The places don't forget like people do. They stew. They absorb. They wait. Not vengeful. Not even angry.

Just heavy with memory and mildew, breathing slow beneath fresh coats of paint. She thought of Velu. His burnt body. The bruises no one had wanted to see. The trail that ended not in a blaze, but in a whisper. They'd written the report. Filed the death. Dismissed the man.

But the ground?

The ground had kept the receipt. Somewhere below the new flooring. Beneath the tiles, the laminate, the gloss. Under the footfall of residents who'd never asked what came before

Story of the Storey

their dreams started twitching, the ground still remembered.

Maybe that was the real story. Maybe Velu wasn't the beginning. Maybe he was just the part the place that decided not to digest. Not this time.

Mira closed the laptop. The comment stayed on the screen long after the machine went dark.

For thirteen full minutes, the CCTV feed went static. It was not black or not disconnected. Just a restless fuzz, like snow on an old television. Humming faintly, too faintly to pick up on speakers. When the footage returned, everything seemed normal.

Almost.

The corridor outside Flat 5B looked empty at first. Then frame by frame, they saw her. A nurse or something that had once been one. She didn't walk. She drifted. One foot never quite met the ground, as though she was still deciding whether to belong to it.

Nurse's uniform was faded at the edges, yellowing into the grain of the walls. The white cap on her head sat too still, too stiff. Her face blurred, like it didn't want to be remembered. She glided past the camera. Then she paused and turned. She stared directly into the lens. Just for a moment. Half a second, maybe less. But it was long enough to know she saw.

Then gone.

In the next association meeting, they played the clip. No one laughed. No one reached for their coffee. Even the children, watching from behind plastic chairs, stayed quiet. The usual murmurs about vendors, parking, unpaid dues died in the throat.

Finally, the treasurer cleared his throat and mumbled, "Software glitch, probably." Nobody argued. But nobody deleted the footage either. Someone asked if they should install more cameras. Someone else suggested a priest. The meeting ended without a vote.

The next day, 5B was with white stickers taped over their doorbell. By evening, several flats followed. Just in case.

5B

The voice note arrived at 2:47 a.m.

"It's in the air. In the walls. We never left the place." Shreya whispered. Her voice was brittle, and breath. It was dragging like a torn shoe through gravel. The message was less than ten seconds, but it didn't need to be longer.

She didn't wait for a reply. She didn't type a follow-up. She simply sent it to Srinidhi and disappeared. By 3:10 a.m., her body was found in the bathtub. The water was cold. They are not tepid and not cold.

Despite, the water heater still humming on the wall like a dying insect. Her arms were folded across her chest, as if she were holding herself together. Her hair had fanned out, floating lightly in the water like kelp.

There were no pills. Not even razors. Also, no slit wrists or final notes. Not the kind people leave behind with commas and apologies.

Except the mirror. There, scrawled in shaky lines, was a single message: **NO EXIT.**

Not in steam or lipstick, but in blood. The kind of red that had already darkened, turned rust at the edges. Forensics swabbed it. Confirmed it was hers. But no wounds. No exit wounds, someone joked.

No one laughed.

The report said suicide. The psychiatrist said delusion. The residents said: **God help us.** Srinidhi said nothing. Not at first.

She didn't cry. Not even when she entered Shreya's flat to collect her things. She found the kettle still warm. A half-eaten banana. A tiny crack in the bedroom wall that hadn't been there before. She walked into the bathroom, stood in front of the mirror, and looked at the dried message.

NO EXIT.

She listened to the voice note again and again. By the seventh time, she whispered along.

"It's in the air. In the walls. We never left the hospital."

She called no one. She just started writing. She remembered Shreya sending her the paper cuts of death in her chats.

At first, it was for herself. Notes. Patterns. Names. She scribbled in a small green notebook she kept under her mattress. In all caps: **BEFORE POWER CUT – NORMAL – AFTER POWER CUT – DIFFERENT**

She listed it all:

1. The grandfather's fever

2. Anjali's fall

3. The ants

4. The dreams

5. The nurse

6. Vishwa

7. then Shreya.

She walked into the police station. While entering, Srinidhi smelled of sweat and metal filings. The fan overhead chopped the air into nervous slices.

The writer didn't look up. "We already filed it," he said, rifling through a file. "No foul play."

"You didn't listen to the message."

"Lady, you want the recording back, file an RTI."

A creak at the door.

"Whom are you asking to file an RTI?" said a low voice from behind.

The writer looked up and stiffened as Sub-Inspector Ravi stepped into the room, removing his sunglasses, too slowly for this hour of the evening. His badge caught the yellow light, glinting like a judgment. He looked once at Srinidhi, then broke into a smile.

"Well. If it isn't Mira Sen herself."

The room tilted slightly.

SI Ravo continued, "Mira Sen aka Srinidhi. Her detective name." When she and Ravi parted ways in the Velu murder case a few months before. It happened when she believed investigations had answers. SI Ravi and Mira were asked to surrender the case.

The writer's face drained of colour. "Sorry, ma'am," he muttered. He suddenly found it difficult to breathe with his tie still on.

Srinidhi nodded. Her eyes were unreadable. She placed the green notebook on the desk. Opened to a page covered in what looked like mathematical loops but were really timelines. Dates. Floor numbers. Symptoms. Disappearances.

She let the silence stretch. Let the ceiling fan buzz grow heavier, as if time itself was watching.

"We're all still inside it," she said softly.

Ravi had been checking his phone. He paused. Looked at her.

"Inside what?"

"The hospital. Or clinic. Or something related to the medical world," she said.

"Not the real one. The one that was here before. Before they razed it. Before they built Sunrise Residency. The structure may have changed. But the walls remember."

He stared. Not blinking. Not scoffing either.

"People don't vanish, Ravi. Not like this. Not by accident. Not in patterns."

She pointed at the loops.

"There are sleep disruptions, hallucinations, spatial distortion and behavioural breaks."

"The girl in the bathtub?" Ravi asked.

"She saw too much," Srinidhi replied. "Not enough."

Ravi exhaled, eyes flicking to the window behind her, as if hoping something out there would make all this sound less like madness.

"What do you want us to do?"

"Reopen the case," she said.

"This isn't over. Not by a long shot."

Ravi said nothing. The writer scratched behind his ear and cleared his throat.

"We could... I mean, maybe cross-check some, "

"Reopen the case," she repeated. She didn't shout. But her voice landed like a stamp.

Later that evening, her doorbell rang twice.

No one was there.

But when she looked through the peephole, for a split second, she thought she saw a flash of white. A uniform, or a trick of the light. She didn't sleep that night. She pressed play on the voice note again. One more time. Let it play into the dark.

Chapter 5: Buried with Intention

The morning didn't begin in a delightful way. Neither of them had slept properly. Ravi was the kind of man who slept like a streetlamp, flickering on and off with every thought. Srinidhi sleep habit of deserting her the closer she got to something real.

As per yesterday's plan, Srinidhi and SI Ravi met at their usual coffee shop. It was a cramped corner. Neither mentioned how tired they looked. Ravi stirred his coffee absently. His eyes scanning the street beyond. Srinidhi stared into hers like it held a prophecy she wasn't ready to read.

They didn't speak much. There wasn't any need. By now, silence was their shared language. One that held all the things they didn't yet know how to say.

"Sub-Registrar Office opens at ten," Ravi said.

Finally breaking the quiet, tapping his watch even though it wasn't yet nine.

"But if we wait near the tea cart long enough, someone always opens the gate early."

She nodded, standing without finishing her coffee.

The day hadn't begun. It was merely waiting to be acknowledged. They left the coffee shop without fanfare, no lingering goodbyes to the waiter, no backward glances.

The city was already stretching into its weekday rhythm: autos weaving through potholes, newspaper bundles tossed like careless promises, the scent of jasmine mixing with exhaust.

The Sub-Registrar's office wasn't far. They walked most of the way in silence, Ravi slightly ahead, Srinidhi matching his pace. Her dupatta tugged occasionally by the wind like it was trying to pull her back.

By the time they reached the tea cart just outside the rusting gates of the office. The sun had climbed halfway up a stubborn sky. The tea vendor recognized Ravi with a nod. Maybe not by name, but by the pattern of routine.

Ravi ordered two glasses without asking. Srinidhi didn't protest. They stood there, the steam curling between them, watching the blue shutters of the registrar office as if waiting for something more than just iron to give way.

Across the road stood the building. It was pale-yellow, weathered, and with fading red letters. Under an iron arch that read *SUB-REGISTRAR OFFICE – ZONE VIII, CHENNAI.*

Two men were already arguing near the entrance. One held a crumpled folder, the other a helmet and a complaint. They finished their tea in silence, and when the gate creaked open with a slow, metallic groan, they walked through.

Inside the office, Ravi moved to the counter with practiced ease.

"We need the Encumbrance Certificate for Plot No. 143/A, Sunrise Residency area. Full chain of ownership."

The clerk looked up without much interest. "Application forms on the desk. Fill it. Select duration. You want complete history?"

"From as far back as you've got," Ravi said.

He was flashing a laminated ID card. "Police background check." With a grunt, the man pulled a register closer and scrawled something inside.

"Go to Counter 3 for digital EC. But if you're tracing old paper records, that'll be upstairs. Archives. Ask for the mother document. Survey number, sub-division, prior document number, all that will be listed there."

"Do we sign somewhere?" Srinidhi asked. The clerk didn't look up. "On your way back. Upstairs first."

They climbed the stairs slowly. Ravi whispered, "If this country ever wants to bury the truth, it just needs to misfile it by one digit." The archive room was dim, cool. Racks of files stretched into silence.

A few men moved like monks, torches in hand, brushing dust off bureaucratic scripture. It took twenty minutes, one cold soda, and a promise of "just a scan, no taking originals" before a man retrieved a file from a rack labelled *"Pre-2015 Registrations – Zone VIII."*

He dropped it in front of them with a thud that startled a pigeon from the rafters. The mother document was partly handwritten, partly typed. Tamil and English merged, interrupted by legalese, official seals, and faded red stamps. Srinidhi's eyes scanned hungrily. Then:

> *"Property originally registered under Arunava General Hospital Trust, 1976, for public health purposes, including OP block, maternity, psychiatric, and research units."*

She sat back. "Not a clinic," she said. Ravi scratched his chin. "A full hospital."

She turned the page. A scribbled note gave the reason for sale: "Deemed surplus due to Metro Line 5 acquisition." Then beneath, in smaller writing: *"Main hospital building unaffected. Land decommissioned under revised civic health norms."*

Srinidhi shook her head. "That's a cover story. The metro only needed one edge. They sold the whole land."

Ravi was quiet, staring at the sketch stapled at the back, a new building plan overlaid on an old hospital outline.

Outside, the sunlight felt too sharp, the street too new. Srinidhi paused at the gate, staring back at the building. For a moment, she felt she was walking over something that hadn't agreed to stay buried.

Behind her, the archive window snapped shut. They didn't speak much as they crossed the city to reach the CMDA office. They only exchanged glances when their phones buzzed with a reminder: *"Next step – planning permissions."*

The Chennai Metropolitan Development Authority building loomed impersonal, concrete under concrete skies. Here, the past wasn't just archived, it was redesigned. Inside, the air smelled of paper and ink and systems that didn't like being questioned.

Ravi walked up to the enquiry desk. "We're looking for the sanctioned plan for Plot No. 143/A. Sunrise Residency. If there's a revised building plan or planning permission file attached to it, we need those too."

The clerk barely looked up. "Online portal," he said.

"We already checked," Srinidhi said. "Half the files are watermarked 'upload pending.'"

He sighed and motioned them to a counter behind a glass pane. After a brief shuffle of forms and token numbers, they were handed a plastic sleeve containing photocopies. "Sanctioned in 2080." The woman at the desk said. "Original plan shows two towers, twenty floors, standard setback, approved height."

Ravi held the papers up to the light. "No mention of the old hospital?"

"Not in this version." She shrugged. "The land use was changed in 2083. Marked as mixed residential-commercial after decommissioning. Any previous civic use isn't our jurisdiction."

"What about revised plans?"

She flipped through a logbook. "Hmm. Revised proposal in 2085. Approved same year, under fast-track multi-storey housing scheme."

Srinidhi leaned in. "What changed?"

"Added two extra floors. Basement plan altered. Rear service corridor reduced."

Ravi's brow furrowed. "Any objection filed?"

The woman hesitated. "There's a remark here. Objection raised; file attached. But the attachment's not here."

"Not uploaded?"

"Maybe lost. Maybe 'missing.' Happens sometimes."

Ravi exhaled. "Can we file a requisition?"

"You can. Won't get it today."

Srinidhi held up the site layout from the revised plan. "This basement design of Ruby towers, it overlaps the area marked in the hospital blueprint as psychiatric research. It's not just reduced. It's erased."

"Could be an error," the clerk offered weakly.

"Or a rewrite," Srinidhi said. "Not of plans. Of memory."

They left with copies of what they could collect. Outside, the sun had slipped into a haze. Ravi glanced at the sky.

"Everything above ground looks so sure of itself."

Srinidhi folded the blueprints slowly. "It's the foundations that lie."

They left the CMDA office with the photocopies clutched in their hands, the weight of the file pressing down on them like something still unspoken.

Ravi flipped through the pages as they walked toward the car. The faint hum of the city surrounded them, but the world felt distant, as if the noise couldn't reach them anymore.

Ravi stopped just before getting into the car. He paused over a specific page in the revised plan. He traced the outline of the building on the map. His finger running over the edges with an intensity that made Srinidhi pause beside him. "The layout has changed," he said, more to himself than to her.

Srinidhi leaned over, looking at the map. Her eyes followed the lines carefully, noting the placement of the towers, the pathways, the service areas. "The plan shows Ruby tower is now on the East side." She pointed. "That wasn't the original placement."

"Exactly," Ravi said, rubbing his chin. "In the old hospital plan, the spot where Ruby Tower is now, it used to be on the West side. But in the new plan, they've moved it to the East."

He pointed to the blueprint. "And see this? The main gate, which everyone uses to enter the complex, is now on the North side. Earlier, it faced another direction."

Srinidhi frowned. "So they've changed the entire layout?"

Ravi nodded. "Yes. They didn't just build something new—they've turned everything around. The towers, the gate, the paths. They've done it so that no one would recognize what this land used to be. They wanted to erase all traces of the hospital."

Srinidhi felt a shiver run through her. "So they moved everything. Even the entry points. Why would they do that?"

Ravi squinted at the map, his thoughts moving quickly. "They want it to be unrecognizable. Everything that used to tie this land to its past, its history... wiped away. Changing the gate, changing the towers, it's all part of making sure no one remembers what was here."

"But why Ruby tower?" she asked. "Why that one specific spot?"

Ravi's expression hardened. "It's not just a shift. It's strategic. They've placed her tower exactly where the old psychiatric and research wing once stood."

He flipped through the rest of the document, comparing the old map with the new one.

"The foundation of that building is probably still here, hidden under these new plans. They've buried something, and I'm betting it's more than just bricks."

Srinidhi stepped back, her mind running through the possibilities, piecing together the fragments of history, the subtle erasures that had happened right under their noses.

The gate at the North. The tower on the East. Shreya's memories, her past, now locked away behind concrete walls and new facades.

"They didn't just build over it. They redesigned it," she said quietly. "They've erased everything." Ravi nodded slowly, a frown tugging at his lips. "Someone's made sure the right people forgot. It's not just buried. It's buried with intention."

They both stood in silence for a moment, the weight of the plan settling around them like a final truth. The landscape had shifted, and in the process, so had their understanding of what had been lost.

Srinidhi's fingers were cold as they slipped the mother document back into her bag, the edges of the file crinkling under her touch. She folded the papers tight, as if they might try to escape, scattering secrets she wasn't yet ready to face.

Her mind, though, was already far ahead, lost in the threadbare fragments of what they had just uncovered. Ravi was already a few steps ahead. He was muttering about the lack of decent public washrooms and the curious absence of decent lunch spots in the area.

But none of that mattered to her now. Her thoughts had broken from his rhythm. She kept seeing that name.

Selva.

It wasn't the name of a trustee or a director or anyone with any significant power. It was just a name, hastily scrawled in the margins. It tucked away in the corners of the document like it didn't belong. But the more she thought about it, the more it felt like it belonged too much.

Under the heading "Caretaker, residential quarters, non-medical staff," she found it again. "Selva (temporary appointment, inherited duty)."

The words "inherited duty" caught her attention like a thorn, digging into her thoughts.

It felt so out of place, as if the phrase had somehow wandered into the wrong document. It was like an anachronism, an oddity in a place that had otherwise been so neatly scrubbed of history.

She turned the page slowly, her gaze falling on a new sheet, a tracing of the building's layout, this one with the faintest pencil markings. At the corner, she saw it again. A name. Written in careful, deliberate script: *Selva.* "*Quarter 3 / Utility Access / Key-holder: Selva (lineage occupant, no formal pay grade).*"

Lineage occupant. The words stuck in her mind, haunting in their oddness. There was something deeply human about the phrase, like a thread to a past that refused to be severed.

Someone had gone to great lengths to erase the legacy of the hospital, but the ink on these pages was stubborn. The names, the titles, the history it refused to disappear entirely. A whisper of the past that clung to the present.

Ravi's voice broke her focus. "Are we going to Selva's place or what?"

She blinked, shaking herself free from the web of thoughts that had already begun to tie themselves into knots. The name was there, and so was the mystery, but now, they needed to find the man himself.

"Let's go," she said, her voice quieter than she intended, still tangled in the shadows of the words on the page. "Let's find Selva."

Chapter 6: Footsteps on Forgotten Soil

Selva lived at the edge of what was now a half-built commercial zone. It is in a fading single-story house whose roof bore more rust than tile. The gate was wooden and barely hanging on. A cow was tethered to the side, flicking its tail as if bored with the entire world.

He opened the door with the face of someone who expected no one and preferred it that way. Long white beard, a vest that looked older than any official document she'd touched, and skin tanned so deep it had its own memory of the sun.

"Yes?"

His voice wasn't unfriendly. But not interested either.

"I'm looking for information about Arunava General Hospital."

He didn't react.

"It used to be here. The northeast wing, psychiatric and research."

Still no flicker. "I found your name," she added. "On a register. It said you lived on the grounds. That you... inherited the role." This time, his eyes moved. Not to her, but toward the neem tree in his front yard.

"Selva," she pressed gently. "Do you remember anything?"

He didn't answer. He turned and went inside. She waited. It was long enough to be uncomfortable but not long enough to leave. Finally, he came back. No files. No boxes. Just a sentence.

"Don't speak of the land," he said softly, almost to the neem tree. "Let the ground keep its own silence. It remembers what we forget."

Srinidhi blinked. "What does that mean?"

He didn't answer. Instead, he stepped off the porch and pointed vaguely to the plot across the lane.

"You see apartments now," he said. "But before… you couldn't build. The soil used to give way, not all at once. It was happening slowly, foot by foot. A wall would stand and then lean without touching. Lights would go off even when the wires were new."

She shivered, though the heat hadn't changed. "You lived there?" she asked.

"My great-grandfather owned it," he said. "Him and his brothers. They built a small clinic. Then it grew. Became a hospital."

"What happened?"

"Two brothers died young. Their sons took over. Then came COVID. You could have heard from your ancestors"

Srinidhi didn't answer.

"They all went in one wave. My grandfather was thirty when it happened. He was the only one left, fifth son of the fifth son. So they made him caretaker. Not legal heir. Just... witness. To what was."

"You?"

"I'm just what came after. I didn't choose this house. It outlasted the people who could afford to move."

She looked toward the plot. The one with Tower C now jutting awkwardly into the space that used to be the northeast wing. The one with broken elevator lights, and tenants who left without telling why.

"Do you have any documents?" she asked.

He looked back at the house. "Not with me."

Her heart sank.

"They're under the Pooja Shelf," he said, finally.

"In the storeroom. Wrapped in turmeric cloth. He said if someone asked, and they asked right, give it. Only once."

Srinidhi followed him into the house. The inside smelled of old rice and camphor. Dust didn't settle here; it mingled, suspended like a secret. He took a flat crowbar and pried open the corner of a warped tile.

Beneath it, a metal box. He didn't rush. Every

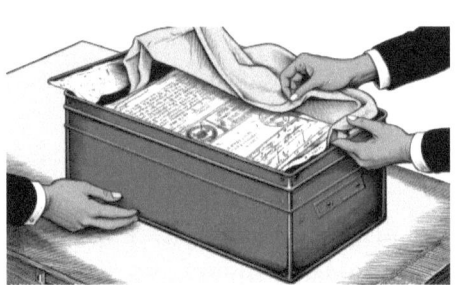

movement was deliberate, reverent. The cloth was yellowed but intact. Inside, papers. Typed, handwritten, stamped, smudged. She didn't even know where to look first.

"Take it," he said.

"You don't want to know why?"

"I already do," he said.

She hesitated, then: "Did you ever go inside that wing? The northeast one?"

A pause.

"Once," he said. "By mistake."

"And?"

"There was no silence in that ward," he murmured.

"Even with no one inside, the air made sounds. Like it wanted to say something but had no mouth."

She stood still. Her hand rested on the lid of the metal box, papers half-folded, turmeric cloth brushing against her wrist like a sleeping thing. The moment held weight, not a climax, but a shift.

Srinidhi cleared her throat. "Would it be possible to make copies of these?" Selva looked at her with the flat softness of a man who'd buried more than just family. "You came with a police officer?"

"Yes," she nodded. "Sub-inspector Ravi. He is assisting me."

He didn't nod. He didn't even blink. He simply turned and gestured toward the bundle. "Then take them. The copies you need can be made by someone who understands the risk of touching old things. I don't want to see these papers again."

She opened her mouth to protest. Out of habit, politeness, disbelief, but the look on his face made her swallow the words. It wasn't indifference. It was relief masquerading as distance.

Like someone handing off a stone they'd been made to carry for decades. Outside, the neem tree rustled with a breeze that wasn't there a moment ago.

Chapter 7: Not all the dreams are dreams

Back on the main road, the city resumed its muttering. Honks, feet, the hiss of bus tyres against a road that had been resurfaced four times in six years. Srinidhi turned toward the south side, where Sunrise Residency jutted out like a crooked molar from the residential layout, unfinished enamel and all.

The side gate creaked as she entered. Two women stood nearby with half-dry clothes and plastic clips in their mouths. Their elbows poked out like wary antennae. One of them squinted at her.

"You looking for flat?" the woman asked. "One just got empty last week. Corner side. No sunlight."

"I'm not looking to rent," Srinidhi said, flashing her ID but not mentioning Ravi yet. "I'm doing a survey. About previous land ownership."

"Eh?" the second woman frowned.

"All that was long time ago. Builder said everything legal. Bhoomi puja and all done. We even got coconut prasadam."

"I understand," she said. "I just need to speak with someone who's lived here since the beginning. Or at least knows the stories people tell." That phrase worked better than expected.

They fetched Raghavan, third-floor tenant, leg brace, chess player, memory hoarder. He came down slow, like he knew how stories liked to ferment. They seated her on a cement bench near the half-grown Ficus. Someone had tied a yellow thread around its trunk, maybe for safety, maybe to say sorry. It wasn't clear.

"People come and go," Raghavan said. He was carefully folding his towel like it was something important. "But the ground remembers. Every September, our drains clog. Not regular clogging thick black sludge, smelling like burnt turmeric and copper wires.

"Did you ever see the land before construction?" she asked.

"No," he said. "But my nephew did. He was on a survey team in 2080. Said there were walls. Half gone. Tamil letters scratched backwards. A tree that bloomed only at night. He didn't stay long."

She jotted this, hand moving faster than her thoughts.

"Any complaints from tenants?" she asked. "Power surges? Water irregularities?"

"Not irregularities," Raghavan said. "Rhythms. Like the building has moods."

She paused.

"There are days," he continued, "the lift doesn't come when called. They were not stuck or not broken. They were just absent. Then there are flats where people hear dripping, but there are no taps. No plumbing in that wall."

She felt a stretch inside her. The kind that happens when something doesn't want to be understood in pieces.

"Do you remember when construction began?"

"2081 maybe. The land passed into the builder's hands in 2079. Officially. Unofficially... nobody really knows who signed what."

That tracked with Selva's documents.

"They rushed the first two towers. Completed by 2085. But then something happened. Quietly. Nothing in the papers. Just a hush."

"What kind of hush?"

"The kind that moves people sideways. Workers left. Cement mixers sat idle. Third tower's foundation was poured, but nothing rose from it.

Some say they found bones. Others say something older sealed metal, not rusted, like it had waited."

"And?"

"They wrapped it up in tarpaulin and lime. Flat. Like burial, but not ritual. Since then, only two towers. The rest drawings on brochures. Families came, stayed, some left. Others endured."

She scanned the balconies. Two towers, just two, standing like exclamation marks in a paragraph that was never finished. She collected contact numbers. Tenants. Maintenance. A former site worker's cousin who "knew someone who drank with the builder once." Every link frayed. But sometimes, frayed threads showed you the loom.

Smriti sits cross-legged near the stairwell, sketching the fogged mirror she once saw in Meenakshi's bathroom. Without needing prompts, she begins to speak.

"They say stories gather in buildings," she says. "And this one has soaked in quite a few."

She remembers Srinidhi too. Shreya's cousin. "We met only twice," she says, eyes fixed on the drawing. "Once during Shreya's housewarming in 2087. The second time... was her burial in September 2089." There's a beat of silence.

Story of the Storey

"Shreya passed away twenty days ago," Smriti finally whispers, "but the shift, it is the real change began long before that. All of it started after that one power-cut."

As Smriti speaks, Srinidhi listens quietly, scribbling notes, piecing together fragments. Smriti continues, her voice low and steady. She starts recounting the strange changes in the apartment after the various power cuts.

Mr. Rajagopal, the cheerful grandfather from 10B, now taps in threes whenever he pauses on wood, on walls, even on people's shoulders.

9B Anjali from 9B, once a vibrant teacher, has taken to sleepwalking and humming a lullaby no one recognizes.

Kumudha's parakeet the one that used to mimic film dialogues flew into the switchboard and disappeared. Since then, Kumudha compulsively touches door handles three times before she enters or leaves a room.

Vishwa, the six-year-old who vanished during hide-and-seek. His giggle still echoes near the trash chute. Ambika, his mother, never switches off the fridge light anymore. "He doesn't like the dark," she says.

Mohan, the joke-cracking neighbour in 2B, now whistles **2B** tunelessly at night. He denies it when asked, but his wife has recordings of him pacing and whistling in the dark.

6C Meenakshi from 6C wakes to her mirror fogged with three concentric circles. They return each time she cleans them.

Many residents began dreaming the same dream: white corridors, Dettol, gloved hands, elevators with no end, and a low, buzzing hum that grows louder with each step.

There were even whispers going around: *"Not all the dreams are dreams."* Sharada's husband began sharing the dream. He wears his watch to bed now, checks door handles obsessively, whispers numbers in the night. "There's no floor under our bed," he murmurs. "Just tile."

Kamini speaks in her sleep in a language that plays backward, like Sanskrit in reverse. Sharada alone dreams the white room. A nurse with too many fingers. A clipboard of unreadable, yet strangely understandable symbols.

"They say what vanished wasn't just a boy. Or Shreya. Or light."

She looks up.

"It was the line between waking and dreaming. I'm sure we didn't move in. We woke it up."

Srinidhi's notebook now bore the weight of more than just observation. It had arrows, arcs, scribbled margins. A page entirely filled with graphite, smeared by a diagonal palmprint as if the act of recording had become urgent, even desperate.

Red ink trailed after names; blue lines connected symptoms to dates. The edges curled slightly, damp with sweat. Srinidhi had stopped writing like a researcher. She was now recording like a witness.

Smriti's voice still lingered in her ears slow, steady, unnervingly calm. "Not all the dreams are dreams," she had said. "Some are replays."

Now, seated on the apartment's terrace with the notebook on her lap, Srinidhi began cross-referencing each case file with the current tenant list. Her fingers moved without hesitation. She didn't need to double-check. The details had embedded themselves too deeply.

9B

Name: *Anjali*
Flat: *9B*
Incident: *Recurrent nightmares*
Details: *Experiences vivid nightmares of endlessly falling while alone. Wakes up screaming "Don't." No history of trauma or phobia of heights.*

Name: *Vishwa*
Flat: *Lived with Ambika*
Incident: *Disappearance during hide-and-seek*
Details: *Previously observed sleepwalking; once found bleeding from both ears. Laughter reportedly still heard near the trash chute.*

Name: *Unknown boy*
Flat: *Tower A*
Incident: *Disturbing drawings and*

> *statements*
> **Details:** *Drew five faceless figures on green beds; said, "They're sleeping until it's safe." One bed consistently drawn empty and circled.*

> **Name:** *Mr. Rajgopalan*
> **Flat:** *Not specified (family friend of a resident's grandfather)*
> **Incident:** *Memory confusion*
> **Details:** *Claimed "2020 had too many echoes." Recalled a man getting an injection and forgetting his name.*

The more she wrote, the more the notebook stopped looking like research. It became a map of reverberations. Srinidhi flipped back to Smriti's words. Her pen hovered.

Smriti's account:

> *We met on 2087 in Shreya's housewarming. Last met her at her burial in September 2089. Recalled seeing Sharada before she started dreaming of the sterile white room. Shared image: nurse with too many fingers, clipboard with unreadable text.*

Note: Smriti never dreamed. But she remembered other people's dreams.

Srinidhi turned the page and began to draw.

A diagram emerged, part floor plan, part neural network. Each apartment unit became a node. She shaded the ones with shared symptoms. Dotted lines for dreamers. Solid lines for the ones who disappeared or had tactile hallucinations. Every incident brings Ruby tower inside the picture. That silence unsettled her more.

A sudden gust lifted the page, fluttered it violently. Srinidhi pressed it down, only to notice the smear on her own palm. The same graphite that had shaded the dream corridors was now on her skin.

In a blank corner, she scribbled, her blog's hook started to fall in line,

Working theory:

> *This is not haunting. This is imprinting. The building is a recorder. People are its cassette tapes. The drop in power didn't start it, it cleared the tape. Now it's playing back everything it's ever absorbed. But some of us... weren't here when it was first recorded. So why are we hearing it?*

She circled that question. Her fingers shook as she drew the final sketch: a nurse, tall and still, standing in a too-white hallway. On her hands six fingers, long and elegant.

In her grip a clipboard. On it, nothing that resembled text. Yet Srinidhi knew what it meant. She didn't write a caption. She just stared.

Somewhere below, in the corridor near 4D, the parakeet squawked a line from an old film. But the voice was wrong. Too slow. Like a cassette melting in heat. Srinidhi, eyes wide, whispered to herself:

"It's not just echoes. It's rewinding."

The final line in Srinidhi's notebook for that night read: **"We didn't move in; we woke it up."**

She paused after writing it. Her fingers hovered over the words, then drifted away like they feared to underline it. The page felt heavier somehow, as if ink had weight, and truth, even more so.

For a moment, she just stared at her own handwriting. Each letter looked like it had been written by someone else. Someone watching. Someone certain. She closed the book.

The soft *snap* of its cover felt louder than it should have. Around her, the room was still. Still enough to hear the slow tick of the wall clock. The rustle of curtains not touched by wind. Her breath. She stood up to turn off the light. The ceiling fan above hummed a flat, tired tune. But something caught her eye. The mirror.

It stood on the opposite side of the room, half-lit by the lamplight. She hadn't looked into it directly all evening. But now her reflection stared back. Familiar. Tired. Except... something was off. She stepped closer.

There right through the left eye of her reflection was a thin, almost invisible crack. A single line. A hairline fissure that hadn't been there before. She touched her face. Nothing.

She touched the mirror. Cool glass, slightly moist from the night air. But the crack remained. Still and stubborn. It wasn't a scratch on the surface; it was in the glass itself. As though the mirror hadn't shattered from impact but from pressure. From within.

Her breath caught. She leaned in. Her eye, split by the fracture, now looked doubled. She didn't scream. She couldn't. She simply turned away. That night, she tried to sleep with her back to the mirror, the notebook shut tight beneath her pillow like a talisman. It was sometime after 2:00

a.m. when she finally drifted off, the remnants of Smriti's words still echoing in her ears:

"Not all the dreams are dreams, some are replays."

Somewhere between 2:46 and 2:47 a.m., a voice note played. No phone had been touched. No apps opened. There were no notifications. The screen remained dark. Yet the sound emerged soft at first, then chillingly clear.

It was Shreya's voice. Whispering. Just above a breath. The words came slow, strained. Like they were being remembered from a different time or spoken through something else entirely.

"It's in the air. In the walls. We never left the hospital."

Srinidhi sat bolt upright in bed. Her heart pounded like it was trying to crack her chest open. She reached for her phone, but the lock screen didn't show a missed call, a message, nothing. The phone didn't even show any recorded voice playing or anything playing. It was empty, no recent files were opened. She checked the time: 2:47 a.m.

The same timestamp that kept repeating in her scribbles. The same time the boy from Tower A once claimed the "beds started shaking." The same time Mr. Rajkumar had once stood in the corridor muttering, "They're changing the wallpaper again. Green. Green like the old gowns."

Srinidhi threw the covers aside and turned on every light in the room. Even the crack in the mirror now seemed deeper. She approached it cautiously, expecting to see her face. But what stared back wasn't just hers.

The light caught the fissure in such a way that it bent the reflection. Her eye where the crack passed seemed to shimmer, distort. Like it was blinking a beat later than the other.

She backed away. By the time dawn began to seep through the curtains, she had written five new pages in her notebook. Not neat, not structured just bursts of thought. Sketches, numbers, phrases she didn't remember hearing before.

"Sound travels. Memory rides it. The mirror broke because it finally saw. We are the discharge from an old machine."

One final line, written with trembling hands before the sun fully rose: *"Shreya died in 2089. But she keeps whispering."* After reaching home, she didn't go back to sleep.

Instead, she walked to the mirror again. Stared at the fracture. She saw something she didn't expect. Not her own eye and not even a face. Just a flicker. A pulse. As though the glass was breathing or maybe, just maybe, something behind it was.

Chapter 8: The Past That Won't leave

The spoon clinked against the ceramic in a stutter, metal on chipped glaze. Srinidhi had stirred her coffee for three full minutes without taking a sip. The foam had collapsed. The liquid had gone lukewarm. Still, her hand moved, slow circles, as if rhythm could disguise the wrongness growing behind her eyes.

"...You said it *played itself?*"

Ravi leaned forward, a bit too quickly, sending the steel tumbler clinking against the edge of the chipped saucer. "Yes," Srinidhi replied, not looking up from her notebook. "2:46 a.m. again. Always that minute. Like it has a pulse."

The fan overhead made its usual *trrrr-trrrr-trrrr* noise. It was failing to stir the still heat of the room. The café smelt of boiled milk, dust, and turmeric oil from the kitchen. Someone in the back had a burn, probably, or wanted to prevent one. Everything here felt just slightly burnt. The chairs, the sugar at the table edge, her nerves.

Ravi scratched his head, not out of confusion but habit. The gesture of a man who once believed crime followed logic. Who believed sunrise would mean something. He had a little crescent of sweat at the base of his throat, glinting like a moon that didn't belong to any sky.

"No app," she said again, voice quieter.

"No file. No Shreya."

He let that name hang between them. Didn't touch it. Outside, the street looked like any other Chennai morning a boy chasing a bottle cap near a gutter, a man selling plastic roses from a too-small basket, traffic leaning on its horns like elbows on a bar.

"Okay. Say I believe you," Ravi muttered, though his eyes said he was trying. "Say something *is* repeating this... sound, this *thing*... why now? What changed?" Srinidhi let the silence answer him.

Then she added, "What if the question isn't *why now*, but *why us*?" Her fingers trembled. She clenched her fist, then unclenched it too fast. He didn't answer. Because they both knew. Both felt the edge of it, too sharp to touch without bleeding.

"I keep thinking," she said, pushing the sugar pot back and forth between her palms like a pendulum, "of what Rajkumar said before he went quiet again. The injection. The forgetting. Then he asked me if 2020 was still happening."

"You think he meant the pandemic?"

"No. I think he meant the walls. The way they breathe when no one's looking. I think... we live in a place built on the residue of something else. That residue doesn't forget."

Ravi leaned back in his chair and looked like he might laugh. But didn't. He sipped his coffee. Instead, winced, it was mostly decoction and something slightly bitter, like roasted regret.

"You want me to go to my superiors and tell them the buildings are haunted by medical memories? That the walls have *PTSD?*"

She didn't respond. Just pulled a photo from her folder and slid it across. A drawing with green beds, no faces, just bodies and beds.

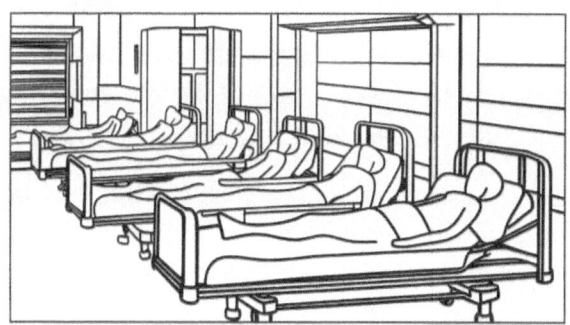

The boy in Ruby tower. He is seven years old. He never saw a hospital. Also, never went in one. But he drew it. Repeatedly. Same layout with same shade of green.

Ravi stared longer than he meant to. Ravi questioned, no one said anything about this. How did you land on this information?

"Sometimes you forget I am private detective who use to help you with case by providing information. I find them through various sources. I verified them with my knowledge." Srindhi gave him a reply.

"This is your theory? Some sort of psychic infection?"

She didn't answer. Instead, she looked out the window at a crow tearing at a crushed juice box. *"I just think,"* she said, almost to herself, *"maybe the hospital never left. Maybe the building grew over it like a scab. And now, someone's scratching it."*

Something in Ravi's stomach twisted. Not fear exactly. But recognition. Like the echo of a lie he once told himself about order.

A waiter came over with the bill. Neither of them reached for it. Ravi pulled out his phone. Checked the call logs, the recordings, everything. Again. Still nothing.

"You said the mirror cracked too?"

Srinidhi nodded. "Hairline. Right through the eye of my reflection. It wasn't broken when I went to sleep." He shook his head slowly, half in disbelief, half because his brain was trying to fit jigsaw pieces that didn't belong to the same picture. "So what now?" he said. "What are we doing with this?"

She finally closed the notebook. "We follow the wrong patterns. Not just the crimes, but the symptoms. We go back to the boy's drawings. Let us go through case and the names."

"That's not going to hold in court."

"I'm not building a case," she said. "I'm looking for the leak."

That stilled him, not a haunting. It is not a ghost. A leak. A disturbance in something supposedly sealed. Like the way a memory surfaces when a smell enters the room, without warning, without logic, without invitation.

Outside, the sun was now high and obscene. It coloured the pavement in such a way that the café's shadow looked bruised. Ravi stood up, but stayed silent for a beat longer than needed. Then he said:

"Next time we meet, I want you to bring that mirror photo. Your sketches. All of them."

She nodded and as he stepped outside, she stayed back. Not to finish her coffee.

But to draw something else. Something she hadn't yet admitted she remembered. Something without faces. This time, the beds weren't green. They were grey and empty.

Later that morning, Ravi stood, the half-drunk coffee forgotten. He didn't speak as he walked to his Bolero. "Get in," he said when Srinidhi followed, already starting the engine.

The wind from the half-open window slapped Srinidhi's cheek like it knew what she was about to find. Or maybe it was just the Chennai sun being its usual bastard self, harsh and full of secrets.

Chapter 9: Paper Trails and Ghost Walls

Inside the Connemara Library, the atmosphere felt like a time capsule. Comfort was not its purpose. It is safeguarding secrets in plain sight was. Srinidhi entered as if chasing a shadow. Ravi followed, quieter, a question awaiting an answer.

"No, not this one. Too clinical," Srinidhi muttered.

She was squatting by a teak shelf marked "Medical Histories 1990 to 2030." A fresh paper cut throbbed on her index finger. The souvenir from a mis-filed journal. She sucked the cut, eyes scanning yellowing titles with restless urgency.

Ravi paced, snapping and unsnapping his leather watchband.

"You said the title starts with Beyond, right?" she asked, still searching.

"*Beyond the Walls*," he confirmed.

He was tugging at the metal drawer of the card catalogue. The rusted roller squeaked.

"I only glimpsed the cover when Ravi scanned it," he added. "Handwritten title. Black ink. Ruled paper slipped inside."

Srinidhi stood, dusting her palms on her kurta. Coffee lingered on her breath. Her stomach tightened with forbidden anticipation.

"Why would researchers hide their names?" she wondered. "Maybe they never did. Maybe someone erased them," Ravi replied.

Behind a bound *Tamil Nadu Health Systems Survey* they found a slim paperback. Its spine was cracked, pages curling in protest. Srinidhi eased it out like something alive.

The once-white cover had faded to sallow beige. Across the top, blocky black marker read:

BEYOND THE WALLS

First Edition Self-Published

Near the corner, pencilled words whispered: "Only two printed." Ravi squinted.

"Two? That is not a print run. That is a secret."

As Srinidhi lifted the brittle cover, a slip of paper slid free. She caught it mid-fall: typed, yellowing, perfect margins.

Srinidhi adjusted her glasses. Her fingers tracing the faded ink on a patient record from Arunava General Hospital, dated 2003. The name 'Sheela' was scrawled at the top. It followed by notes detailing her compulsive tapping behaviour.

> *"Sheela, 2003, compulsive tapping,"* she murmured, her voice barely above a whisper.

Ravi leaned in, comparing it to a more recent file. "Rajagopal, 2086, exhibited similar tapping behaviour before his untimely death." They continued cross-referencing. The parallels between the two sets of patients becoming increasingly evident.

The more they read, the more it felt like the past wasn't gone. It had simply lingered, its echoes seeping into the present through these records.

Set 1: Arunava General Hospital Patients (1999–2009)

1. **Sheela** – Compulsive tapping
2. **Meera** – Persistent humming
3. **Mira** – Fear of darkness
4. **Angel** – Insisted on keeping lights on
5. **Fathima** – Shared dreams with another patient
6. **Bama** – Shared dreams with Fathima
7. **Urmila** – Compulsive humming
8. **Rajesh** – Disappeared during a blackout
9. **Sundram** – Shared dreams with Krishnan
10. **Krishnan** – Shared dreams with Sundram
11. **Joseph** – Compulsive humming

Set 2: Sunrise Residency Residents (2079–2089)

1. **Rajagopal** – Compulsive tapping; deceased
2. **Anjali** – Persistent humming; deceased
3. **Vishwa** – Disappeared during a blackout; deceased
4. **Ambika** – Keeps lights on due to son's fear of darkness; alive
5. **Sharda** – Shared dreams with spouse; alive
6. **Sharda's Husband** – Shared dreams with Sharda; alive
7. **Mohan** – Compulsive humming; alive
8. **Varun** – Teenager who reported seeing the hospital; alive

Story of the Storey

Srinidhi's brow furrowed as she noted the uncanny similarities. "It's as if the behaviours have transcended time, reemerging in a new generation," she said. Ravi nodded; his gaze fixed on the documents. "The patterns are too precise to be mere coincidence."

The room grew silent as the weight of their findings settled in. The past and present were intertwined in a haunting dance, the echoes of Arunava General Hospital reverberating through the halls of Sunrise Residency.

Srinidhi closed the last file, her voice barely audible. "The hospital's history isn't just recorded in these documents; it's alive, manifesting in the residents of Sunrise."

Ravi looked out the library window, the sun casting long shadows over the city. "We need to understand how and why this is happening before more lives are affected.

As they packed up the files, a sense of urgency propelled them forward. The past was not done with them, and the future depended on the truths they were only beginning to uncover.

But before they could leave, one final folder slipped out from the bottom of the stack, different in material, bound in soft leather, aged in a way that suggested it hadn't been opened in decades.

Ravi caught it just in time. Inside, he found the unfiltered notes, not reports, but raw entries. It was the doctors' private record.

"Stop reading it like a report," Srinidhi snapped. "It's not a bloody bank statement." Ravi blinked, lips parted mid-sentence, finger still dragging across the line that had just undone them both. He re-read it, quieter this time, but not less shaken.

> *"The wing was sealed, not evacuated. Patients remained. Records doctored. Incident unreleased."*

"They didn't shut it down. They shut it in."

Srinidhi nodded. Her fingers were twitching again. They were searching for something to hold on to. The pages Selva had handed over were old, brittle, flecked with black mold in the margins. But it wasn't the paper that disturbed her.

Story of the Storey

It was the tone. There was no panic in the report. No outrage. Just methodical, bureaucratic containment. Like you'd list ingredients for a forgotten recipe: three patients sedated beyond response, two with violent recurrence, one missing, presumed untraceable.

Ravi's throat felt dry. "They buried them alive."

"No," she said, voice like rust.

"They buried what they couldn't explain. And they left the rest to rot in silence."

By the time they stepped outside, the world had shifted again. That was not because of what they saw, but because of what they now knew. The hospital wasn't gone. It had only been disguised.

Outside, construction cranes creaked over the old hospital's skeletal remains. Metal moaned. Dust curled up like something waking. The sun was high, but the lot cast its own kind of shadow, one that didn't follow geometry.

Ravi stepped back from the chain-link gate. "The building was destroyed a decade ago. Why now?"

Srinidhi held up a torn blueprint. On the margins, a red marker had circled *Ward 9B*. Over and over. A tight, frantic loop.

"They didn't demolish it. Not really. The new walls stand over old wounds. No salt. No fire. They left the wound to fester."

Ravi wanted to laugh. He almost did.

But the note stapled to the last page said: *DO NOT RETURN TO BLOCK D WITHOUT CLEARANCE. FOLLOW-UP CASES: 0. REPORT CLOSED.*

Follow-up cases: zero. That was a lie. He'd seen them.

She flipped the document to its final page. A handwritten scrawl across the bottom, in ink darker than the printed text:

"The wing's memory will outlive the building. The mind's fracture echoes louder in stillness. You can't knock it down. You breathe it."

There it was, that thud in the chest, the feeling that something had made itself known without a sound. Ravi felt suddenly unclean. Not dirty. *Occupied.* He leaned against the car door. It creaked. The breeze lifted a thin layer of dust from the windshield and dragged it into a curl mid-air before letting it drop.

"What do we do?" he asked. It wasn't rhetorical. It wasn't procedural. It was just tired.

Srinidhi was still staring at the scrawl.

"They destroyed the hospital," she said.

"But no one cleansed the space. No prayer. No ritual. Not even a damn floor wash. Just cement over madness. now,"

"It's leaking," Ravi said. "Into Sunrise."

"No," she corrected, and this time her voice was something like grief. "Into the people. Into children who never knew what this land once held. Into rice cookers, light switches, and bedtime songs. The place isn't haunted. It's *infectious*."

Silence sat between them. Not heavy. Thin, actually. Like it might break if you breathed too loud.

Chapter 10: Truth Must Haunt

Srinidhi sat at her desk. The screen before her glowing coldly. She had a mission to complete: a blog post that would expose the darkness festering within Sunrise Residency.

But as her fingers hovered over the keyboard, an unsettling tension gripped her. She tried to push the flood of emotions out of her mind. The grief, the anger, the memory of her cousin Shreya's death. The reason she was compelled to write in the first place. She had promised herself to remain detached. That is to approach this as a detective, not as a grieving family member.

The building had claimed Shreya's life. She had to ensure that it didn't claim anyone else. Shreya had been vibrant, full of life, until the nightmares started.

It had started small, whispers and strange behaviours that no one had taken seriously until it was too late. The last time Srinidhi had seen her. Shreya was a shell of the person she once was, haunted by something she couldn't escape.

As Srinidhi stared at the blank page, every word felt heavy, like a burden.

How could she talk about it objectively?

How could she expose the darkness without letting it consume her too? She steeled herself.

This wasn't about her. It was about the truth, and the truth needed to be told. Slowly, she began to type, focusing on the cold facts of the case, no emotions, just evidence.

She reminded herself that this wasn't about revenge or retribution. It was about saving others from the same fate. Shreya's death would not be in vain.

The cursor blinked in silence as Srinidhi's fingers tapped the keys, forming the first line of her blog post.

"Sunrise Residency is not a safe place..."

The Unseen Danger at Sunrise Residency
By Srinidhi Sen (Private Investigator)

Sunrise Residency is not a safe place.

I've spent weeks, no, months, studying its history, its residents, and the terrifying patterns emerging from within its walls.

What began as a few odd reports has spiralled into something much darker, more sinister?

This is not just a building; it is a ticking time bomb, a cursed structure that has already claimed lives, and it will claim more unless we act now.

Let me take you through the terrifying reality of Sunrise Residency.

The Disappearances

It started with disappearances, seemingly random, but they all shared the same chilling trait: no one ever saw anything.

One day, a resident was simply... gone. No struggle, no blood, no trace left behind. At first, the police chalked it up to the usual problems, family disputes, runaway cases, but I knew better. Something was wrong.

Take Vishwa, for instance, a young boy who disappeared during a blackout. He was last seen playing in the hallway with his friends, laughing, carefree. When the power went out, his family assumed he had gone to sleep. But when the lights came back on, Vishwa was gone. His room was untouched, and there were no signs of a struggle. His mother, Ambika, claims to hear his voice sometimes, calling from the darkness, but Vishwa never returned.

Then there's Rajagopal, an elderly man who lived with his family on the top floor. He was known for his compulsive tapping on the walls at night, a sound that echoed through the hallways. He died suddenly, his death deemed a natural one by the authorities. But what no one knew was that he'd been whispering about "vaccine."

The Eerie Behaviours

I dug deeper, and I found something far worse than I had anticipated. The remaining residents weren't just suffering from the trauma of these disappearances; they were exhibiting bizarre behaviours, compulsive acts that could not be explained.

Ambika, Vishwa's mother, keeps the lights on all night long, not for herself, but for her son, who once feared the darkness. She says the lights are for Vishwa, as if he's still in the building, trapped in the dark. But I've seen it in her eyes, the fear that he might never leave.

Anjali, a working woman who was found dead in her apartment, had been persistently humming a tune, a lullaby of sorts, just before she disappeared. Her body was found later in an abandoned corner of the building. No one knows what caused her to hum that song endlessly, but it seems as if she was calling for someone, or something.

There's Mohan, a tenant who now compulsively hums day and night. He was a quiet man once, but after the strange incidents began, he too began to hum the same eerie tune that Anjali had. Is it a coincidence, or has the same force claimed him as well?

Then there's Varun, a teenager who lives on the third floor. He's the only one who still talks about the hospital, Arunava General Hospital, that is. No one believes him. They think it's just his imagination. But he insists that he saw it, in the very spot where Sunrise Residency now stands. He claims to have seen the hospital in his dreams and even in the building's shadows. There's no mistaking the connection, he's not imagining it. Something from the hospital's past has followed him into the building.

The Hidden History of Arunava General Hospital

As I gathered more information, something even darker began to emerge. These strange behaviours were not new.

In fact, they had been seen before, decades ago, within the walls of the now-defunct Arunava General Hospital. The residents of Sunrise weren't just reacting to their surroundings; they were being affected by something that had come before them.

Arunava General was a mental health institution, a place where the unexplainable *was dealt with behind closed doors. The hospital had been closed abruptly, and its records were sealed. But the connections were undeniable.*

A significant number of Sunrise's current residents had ties to that institution, either as patients or as family members of those who had once been treated there.

What was most disturbing was the similarity between the behaviours I was now seeing and those exhibited by former patients of Arunava General.

Rajagopal's tapping. Vishwa's disappearance. Anjali's humming. These were not coincidences. They were all echoes of the hospital's grim history, now bleeding into the present.

A Call for Action

Sunrise Residency was a place of beauty once, a luxurious building meant to be a home for many. But now, it has become a place of nightmares. The residents are living in fear, their minds trapped in a spiral of paranoia and confusion. They don't understand what's happening to them, but I do. And I've seen enough to know that this isn't just coincidence. This is something much darker.

If you live in Sunrise Residency, or if you know someone who does, it's time to take this seriously. This building is not safe. There's something inside it, something that has been festering for years. And it will claim more lives if we don't do something about it now.

The authorities have done nothing. The building management has stayed quiet. It's up to us to expose the truth before it's too late.

Srinidhi Sen, Private Investigator

With her fingers hovering over the 'publish' button, Srinidhi paused. A wave of uncertainty flooded her. She had been through so much already, her cousin's death, the chilling discoveries, but this felt like crossing a line. She clicked it anyway. The world needed to know. The time for silence was over.

The moment Srinidhi hit 'send,' something unexpected happened. The silence that followed felt too long, almost suffocating, before her phone began to buzz.

First, a single notification. Then another and another later. It wasn't just a few views; it was an overwhelming flood. The blog post was gaining traction, and fast.

Within hours, it spread across social media like wildfire. People from all corners of the city began sharing it, commenting, and debating its contents.

The eerie details of Sunrise Residency were now public. The darkness she had uncovered wasn't something the city was ready to ignore. Tweets, posts, and hashtags emerged almost instantly, all centred around the building's sinister reputation.

The local news outlets, always hungry for a story with a hint of scandal, jumped on it. Journalists combed through Srinidhi's blog, pulling quotes, dissecting every word.

They interviewed former residents, local experts, and even current tenants who had previously kept quiet about the strange happenings in the building.

The media quickly caught fire, with headlines questioning everything: "Has Sunrise Residency Been a Government Cover-up?" "Are Residents at Risk in Sunrise Residency?" and "Private Detective Exposes a Building's Dark Secrets."

Within 24 hours, the story had broken through the usual news cycle. It wasn't just another sensational headline; it was a disturbing truth that the public couldn't ignore.

The debates began almost immediately. On one side, people rallied behind Srinidhi, applauding her for unearthing what many felt was a long-hidden truth.

There were even a few professionals, psychologists, architects, and urban planners. He who speculated that the building's eerie history could be linked to an unusual energy or environmental factor that affected the minds of the residents.

But on the other side, there were skeptics. Some dismissed Srinidhi as an opportunist, a conspiracy theorist looking to make a name for herself at the expense of an innocent building and its residents. "It's just an old building with problems. Nothing supernatural," they said. "Coincidences."

Despite the criticism, the support only grew. News outlets found themselves diving deeper into the building's past. Interviews with former residents began flooding in, many of whom had experienced unsettling things but had never spoken up before.

The stories poured out, like Ambika's constant fear that her son's spirit was still in the building, or Mohan's obsessive humming that neighbour claimed had started after his inexplicable breakdown.

Story of the Storey

Sharda, who'd never dared to tell anyone about her late-night dreams shared with her husband, was now on air describing her own inexplicable experiences.

As the days passed, it became evident: Srinidhi had touched a nerve. The residents of Sunrise, once quiet and isolated in their own fear, now had a voice. They weren't afraid to use it. One by one, they began to speak up, posting their own testimonies in response to the blog post.

Soon, it wasn't just local residents talking. People from all over the country began chiming in. Other buildings with similar eerie histories, other survivors of strange occurrences, started to share their stories, questioning whether their homes, too, had something darker lurking beneath the surface.

Srinidhi had unwittingly ignited a firestorm, one that was about to spread far beyond what she had ever imagined. Her name, once confined to small investigative circles, was now being whispered across the city, becoming a symbol of the truth-seeker who wasn't afraid to expose what others tried to keep hidden.

But even as the attention continued to build, a chilling thought crossed Srinidhi's mind. She had unleashed something, something far bigger than she had anticipated. She had opened a door, and now, there was no going back.

The ripple that Srinidhi's blog sent through the city had now turned into a wave. At its centre stood the residents of Sunrise Residency.

For years, they had lived with questions. A creaking hallway here, a neighbour whispering to themselves there, children waking up screaming in the night, and a constant, indescribable weight in the air. Everyone had felt it, but no one dared speak.

They had dismissed it as imagination, personal stress, or just the quirks of old architecture. But now, someone had said it out loud. The moment someone named it, everything changed.

Sharda and her husband were among the first to step forward. "We thought we were going mad," she said at a small meeting held in the building's basement. "But it wasn't just us. When I read the blog and saw others describing the same dreams, the same noises, I knew we had to act."

Varun, the teenager who had once mumbled about "seeing a hospital that isn't there," now stood confidently, recounting his vision during the blackout.

Story of the Storey

Ambika, mother of little Vishwa, spoke through tears, describing how her son used to scream at shadows and how she'd kept every light in their flat on ever since his death.

As residents began sharing their stories, a strange sort of solidarity formed. They were no longer alone in their fears. And fear, when shared, often becomes fuel for change.

Legal counsel was consulted. A few residents knew someone in the city council; others began drafting petitions. What started as separate, scattered efforts soon coalesced into a single goal: demolition.

The building, they said, wasn't just faulty, it was cursed. Some were hesitant to use that word, but others embraced it. The evidence, they claimed, wasn't just physical, it was emotional, psychological, and deeply disturbing.

Some residents began to suspect that the site of the old Arunava General Hospital wasn't just beneath the building, it was bleeding through it.

Complaints were officially filed. Dozens of them. From families, individuals, and even a retired school principal who had once dismissed his paranoia as aging. Now, they wanted answers. They wanted safety.

More importantly, they wanted out.

Sunrise Residency was no longer just a home. It was a threat. It's residents, for the first time in a decade, were ready to fight back.

Sub-Inspector Ravi leaned back in his chair, the buzz of the station humming faintly around him. For weeks, he had watched the story of Sunrise Residency unfold. It was first as a curious blog post then as a viral news item, and now, as a stream of people filing into his station with frightened eyes and typed-out complaints.

He had seen it all before, urban legends, exaggerated rumors, and ghost stories spun by bored minds. But this felt different. The faces were real. The fear was real. Most importantly, the facts weren't easily dismissed.

Ravi pulled up the files stacked on his desk, complaints from at least eighteen residents. Different families, different backgrounds, but the same eeriness threading through each account. Humming in the corridors, shadows that moved where they shouldn't, compulsive behaviors, shared dreams, and memories that didn't seem to belong to them.

He opened Srinidhi's blog post again. Her style was methodical, clean. No drama, just data. A detective's eye, not a writer's flourish. She had outlined the timeline of strange events, the tragic deaths, and the buried history of Arunava General Hospital. Something about the precision in her tone made it hard to ignore.

Ravi picked up his pen and began to write. He listed the names of each complainant, tagged similar patterns, and linked incidents to the older case files buried in the department's archives.

A boy named Vishwa, missing during a blackout. Rajagopal, an elderly man who tapped endlessly before collapsing on his balcony. Anjali, who had been humming the same tune for weeks before being found dead in her apartment.

Coincidences don't usually line up this neatly.

By the end of the day, he had done what no one else had dared. He filed a formal FIR combining all the complaints under a single case: **Criminal Negligence and Public Endangerment related to Sunrise Residency.**

It was an unusual charge for an apartment complex. But Sunrise was no ordinary building. This was no ordinary case.

Ravi sent the file to his superior officers with a note: *"Requesting permission for deeper investigation into possible structural, psychological, and criminal anomalies at Sunrise Residency. Media, legal, and civilian pressure high. Action recommended."*

He looked up at the dimming light outside the station window. Something had started. This time, he was not going to let it get buried.

The air in the commissioner's office was thick with protocol. Sub-Inspector Ravi stood straight. He was clutching the case file like a lifeline. It had taken him days to compile, organize, cross-reference the complaints, media reports, and Srinidhi's investigative blog.

He had annotated every point, included transcripts from resident interviews, and even attached floor plans of Sunrise Residency highlighting known hotspots of activity. But what he really carried into that room was conviction.

"The case is unusual," the first senior officer said, flipping through the file. "You're asking for authorization to investigate... what, exactly?"

"Negligence. Psychological distress. Possible criminal concealment of facts during construction. A pattern of behavior too widespread to dismiss."

Ravi's tone was calm, but firm. "What you're suggesting borders on superstition," another official added, raising an eyebrow. "Ghosts in a building?"

"I'm not here to argue about ghosts," Ravi replied. "I'm here to argue about facts. Eighteen formal complaints, four mysterious deaths, one missing child, and mounting public pressure. If we don't move now, we're complicit in the silence."

One by one, he walked the panel through the case. Sharda and her husband sharing identical dreams, Ambika's refusal to turn off lights after losing her son to the dark, the deaths of Rajagopal and Anjali, the viral blog that shook the city, and the growing unrest among citizens.

It was the media coverage that tipped the scale. News clippings flashed across a projector, headlines screaming about public safety, citizen horror, and administrative delay.

His presentation concluded with a simple statement: *"If this were a factory or a school, action would have already been taken. Why not for a place where people sleep every night?"*

The room fell silent.

Approvals were never fast. Forms passed from hand to hand, nods exchanged behind closed doors. But Ravi waited, pacing the halls, making follow-up calls, and chasing signatures. Some officials were reluctant, others wary of being on the wrong side of public outrage.

Three days later, the final stamp came from the department CMDA.

APPROVED: Official inquiry into Sunrise Residency. Structural and psychological evaluation. Possible demolition pending results.

Sub inspector Ravi exhaled for the first time in days. He tucked the signed order into his folder and stepped outside into the sunlit corridor.

Now the truth had permission to come to light. The silence of Sunrise was about to be broken, legally.

Chapter 11: The Wall that Stayed

From the moment Ravi had received the approval, the weight of the task had settled on him like a stone. The inquiry into Sunrise Residency was no longer just another assignment. It was an investigation into the unspoken, the unspeakable.

The words on the paper, "APPROVED: Official inquiry into Sunrise Residency. Structural and psychological evaluation. Possible demolition pending results", had come with both hope and dread. Hope that they might uncover the truth, but dread for what that truth might cost.

He had walked into the offices with the file in his hand, each page heavy with stories of unexplained deaths, shattered families, and growing unrest. But it wasn't just the file that weighed on him; it was the knowledge that whatever was uncovered here, there would be no turning back.

The process began methodically. The files moving from hand to hand. The signatures passed like a ritual. But the silence that followed each query was louder than any answer.

Days passed, each one a blur of meetings, follow-ups, and long, sleepless nights. Ravi had become a shadow in the corridors, chasing the signatures he needed, each official response colder than the last.

Ravi stepped into the Commissioner's office. The signed inquiry order clutched in his hand.

The Commissioner glanced up from his desk, adjusted his spectacles, and nodded once.

"Sub-Inspector Ravi," he said, voice measured.

"We've reviewed the Joint Inquiry Committee's report."

Ravi swallowed, heart hammering. "Sir?"

"The structural audit confirms severe instability in Tower Ruby," the Commissioner continued, tapping the document. "The building is a clear and present danger."

Ravi felt a flicker of relief.

"The CMDA has corroborated unauthorized modifications extra floors, erased service corridors."

The Commissioner leaned back. "We cannot delay. You have my approval to proceed with demolition under Section 256."

Story of the Storey

Ravi's shoulders straightened. "At whose cost, sir?"

"The owners have agreed," the Commissioner replied. "They'll cover demolition and compensation."

Ravi offered a respectful salute. "Thank you, sir. I'll coordinate with the Greater Chennai Corporation team immediately."

He turned to leave, pausing at the door.

"Sub-Inspector," the Commissioner added.

"Document every step. Public safety is paramount, but we must be transparent."

"Understood," Ravi said, determination in his eyes.

As he exited, the weight of the order in his pocket felt like both a promise and a warning—Sunrise Residency's time had finally come.

In the demolition site: Tower Ruby required officers and machines have arrived. Everyone was waiting for one person, The owner of the land, Mr. Arunachalam.

Arunachalam stepped out of his car. He signed the required paper. He turned away from the shadow of the crumbling building. The harsh sunlight casting long lines across his face. His eyes were shadowed, dark, calculating.

He stood there for a moment, looking at the rubble as if the history of that place no longer mattered. The wind blew, rustling the debris, but his voice cut through the stillness with an eerie calmness.

"I thought the loan sharks were the reason," Arunachalam began.

Arunachalam tone far too casual for the weight of his words. "So, I dragged Velu away from here, away from the building. Burnt him. You know, to stop any more trouble, to keep the death quiet." He let out a slow breath, his expression unfazed, as though speaking of a mundane task.

Ravi stiffened, his hand instinctively gripping the edge of the folder in his hand. The words hit him harder than he expected. Though he'd heard rumors, whispers of what might have happened to Velu. But hearing it from Arunachalam himself, the man responsible, sent a chill down his spine.

"But what you don't know," Arunachalam continued. The corner of his lips curling upward, "is that you've smelled the ashes. It wasn't just his body you smelled. It was the end of something far worse. Something I could never have warned you about."

Ravi's mind spun. He had smelled the remnants of a fire, ash, burnt flesh. Something far more sinister. But it wasn't until now that he understood what that smell meant. It wasn't just a simple act of vengeance or self-preservation. It was a sign, a marker of something far more deep-rooted. Something far darker.

He stared at Arunachalam, struggling to suppress the anger that churned within him. "So, it wasn't just about the debt. You had to silence him. Not just for his loans, but for what he knew. For what he could tell."

Arunachalam shrugged nonchalantly, as if discussing a deal gone bad. "People get in the way. People with too many questions. You know how it is, Ravi. Someone has to take the fall. And Velu... well, he was just in the wrong place, asking the wrong questions."

Ravi's breath caught in his chest as the pieces clicked into place. It wasn't just about money. It wasn't just about Velu or his debts. It was about something far bigger, far more dangerous.

The dark secrets buried beneath Sunrise Residency, hidden in the walls, in the very foundation of the place itself. Now, after all this time, it was starting to unravel. The supernatural events, the deaths, the disappearances, all connected to this one twisted moment in time.

Ravi swallowed hard, the weight of the truth pressing down on him. "You think people will just forget?"

Arunachalam's gaze hardened. "They always do. There will be a new residency here. The ghosts of the past? They'll fade into whispers, buried under new construction. Nothing ever stays, Ravi. Nothing ever lasts."

But Ravi knew better now. The ashes of Velu's body weren't just remnants of a man. They were the ashes of something far more terrifying, something that had been born from violence, hidden in the shadows, and now, it was rising. The fear that gnawed at Ravi's insides wasn't just about the past. It was about the future, and the horror that had only just begun.

Chapter 12: Laughter in the cracks

Chennai, 2105, stands as a metropolis transformed. From the years of slow development, the city now boasts a futuristic skyline.

Metro stations, once sparse in 1990, have multiplied across the city, seamlessly connecting its heart to every corner. The trains now run at lightning speed, making a trip to Salem a mere 10 minutes, and Delhi only 40 minutes away by rail.

The streets are bustling with advertisements, larger than life, displayed on towering digital screens. AI has woven itself into every fabric of daily life, from transportation to communication.

The city pulses with energy, as drones zip overhead, delivering goods, and automated vehicles glide through the roads, eliminating traffic jams.

Chennai has become a city of innovation and connectivity, where the old traditions blend with cutting-edge technology. The aroma of Idli and sambar still fills the air, but now, it's alongside the hum of high-speed trains and AI-powered interactions. The change is undeniable, the city is no longer just a place, but a vision of the future.

Story of the Storey

Ruth crossed the familiar bend with her earbuds in and her college bag bouncing lightly at her hip. The old compound wall was gone now, scrubbed from memory like an old chalk mark.

In its place stood a gleaming hoarding: *NEW PLOT COMING SOON – BOOKINGS OPEN.* The font was bold, proud, too clean for this street. She glanced at it absently, her eyes already shifting to the road ahead.

It had been years since she'd walked past this corner without holding her breath, years since she'd tried *that thing*, eyes closed, second step, no sound. She hadn't spoken about it after the second time. No one had asked.

The traffic hummed along, and she kept walking, distracted by a group of schoolchildren shouting across the road. She didn't notice the cluster of sales agents under the white tent across from the hoarding, busy laughing, calling out to potential buyers, waving flyers.

The sun burned low on the horizon, that unsettling kind of dusk again, the kind that doesn't promise an end. She reached the exact spot, the one she always rushed past, and something in the air tightened. Not the kind you see. The kind you feel under your skin. That's when she heard it. A clear voice, female, calm, too calm. "Next."

She froze mid-step. Her breath hitched. The earbuds crackled with some forgotten podcast, but she wasn't listening anymore. Her heart raced ahead of her thoughts. She turned, slow, her skin cold even in the evening heat.

There, from across the road, a sharply dressed woman raised a placard and called again to the couple beside her, "Next, please!"

The sales tent. Not a spirit.

Not a memory. Not *her*. Ruth exhaled sharply; a laugh almost rising but dying halfway. Still, the pressure in her chest didn't leave.

She glanced back once more at the new signboard, then up at the sky. "Some corners," she whispered, "don't let go. Even when you do."

www.ingramcontent.com/pod-product-compliance
Lightning Source LLC
LaVergne TN
LVHW041842070526
838199LV00045BA/1398